JASON

7 Brides for 7 Blackthornes, #2

JULIA LONDON

PRAISE FOR JULIA LONDON

"A passionate, arresting story that you wish would never end." — Robyn Carr, *New York Times* bestselling author

"Julia London writes vibrant, emotional stories and sexy, richly-drawn characters." — Madeline Hunter, *New York Times* bestselling author

"London's characters come alive on every page and will steal your heart."—*Atlanta Journal-Constitution*

"A novelist at the top of her game."—*Booklist*

"London's writing bubbles with high emotion as she describes sexual enthusiasm, personal grief and familial warmth. Her blend of playful humor and sincerity imbues her heroines with incredible appeal."—*Publishers Weekly*

ALSO AVAILABLE

7 Brides for 7 Blackthornes

DEVLIN - Barbara Freethy (#1)

JASON - Julia London (#2)

ROSS - Lynn Raye Harris (#3)

PHILLIP - Cristin Harber (#4)

BROCK - Roxanne St. Claire (#5)

LOGAN - Samantha Chase (#6)

TREY - Christie Ridgway (#7)

OTHER TITLES BY JULIA LONDON

The Princes of Texas

The Charmer in Chaps

The Devil in the Saddle

Highland Groom Series

Wild Wicked Scot

Sinful Scottish Laird

Hard-Hearted Highlander

The Devil in Tartan

Tempting the Laird

Seduced by a Scot

Lake Haven Series

Suddenly in Love

Suddenly Dating

Suddenly Engaged

Suddenly Single

The Cabot Sisters Series

The Trouble With Honor

The Devil Takes a Bride

The Scoundrel and the Debutante

Homecoming Ranch Series

Homecoming Ranch

Return to Homecoming Ranch

The Perfect Homecoming

The Cabot Sisters Series

The Trouble With Honor

The Devil Takes a Bride

The Scoundrel and the Debutante

Lear Family Saga Series

Material Girl

Beauty Queen

Miss Fortune

Highlander Lockhart Series

Highlander Unbound

Highlander in Disguise

Highlander in Love

Over the Edge Series

All I Need is You

One More Night

Fall Into M

Desperate Debutantes Series

The Hazards of Hunting a Duke

The Perils of Pursuing a Prince

The Dangers of Deceiving a Viscount

JASON

7 Brides for 7 Blackthornes, Book 2
© Copyright 2019 by Dinah Dinwiddie
ISBN: 978-0-9993321-3-9

Visit Julia's Website
http://julialondon.com

CHAPTER ONE

ONCE UPON A TIME IN HOLLYWOOD, MALLORY PRICE NEEDED a job.

She was an actress, but admittedly, not a very good one (funny how those high school roles didn't translate into bankable talent as an adult). Her acting gigs were few and far between.

She was also a filmmaker and, if no one minded her saying, a pretty good one. Filmmaking was her passion. But she had only an old used camera, and so far, no one was interested in her short films, in spite of having entered three into various contests around town.

Mallory had run out of money and had to face facts. So she'd combed through job postings for three weeks and the only lead she'd found was "customer service specialist" with the county tax department.

That job had sounded like death on a stick.

Unfortunately, eating was also a personal passion of hers, and she'd been on the verge of taking that really awful sounding tax clerk job. But then, just like in the movies, the heavens had parted and the sun had shone and fortune had smiled its lovely countenance upon her, because she stumbled on an opening for the perfect job.

Mallory was ecstatic. She'd put in her application, and by the time she'd finished folding the laundry, a bot responded to her submission. CALL OFFICE TO ARRANGE INTER-VIEW. So Mallory did. A woman who sounded frazzled and out of breath answered on the fifth ring. Mallory told her why she was calling. The woman said, "Great. Can you come in this afternoon?"

So Mallory raided her roommates closet, found a very cute pink dress, and decided she might as well borrow some shoes, too, and two hours later, she was sitting in the frigid air of the reception area at Blackthorne Entertainment. She felt like a million bucks in Inez's dress and shoes. She felt confident. She was practicing the art of positive thinking, steadying her breathing and chanting her mantra, *I will get this job.*

A woman, about Mallory's age of twenty-eight, suddenly appeared. She had dark hair that she wore in a messy bun—unclear if by design or necessity—a shirt that appeared to have some sort of stain on it, and a pair of jeans ripped at the knees. She had dark circles under her eyes, and without a word, she marched to a desk, picked up an enormous tote, and started shoving things into it. When she had filled it, she hoisted it on to her shoulder and started for the door. That's when she seemed to register Mallory's presence.

She paused. "Are you here for the interview?"

"Yes," Mallory said, and stood up. "I'm Mallory Price." She extended her hand.

The woman made no move to take it. She glanced at the binder Mallory was holding. "What's that?"

"Background material."

The woman blinked. And then burst into laughter. "Good luck with that," she said, and walked out the door.

"But…" Mallory's voice trailed off.

"Are you Mandy Price?" a male asked behind her.

"Mallory." She turned around to the voice and stood, speechless, because the man looking back at her was one of the most gorgeous men she'd ever seen with her own eyes.

He looked her up and down. He scraped at his beard. "Well, come on then. Let's do this." He turned and started walking down the hall.

Her mind leapt to a very strange and sexual place when he said that, but she quickly shrugged it off. "And you are…?"

He barely spared her a glance over his shoulder. "Jason Blackthorne."

Jason Blackthorne. He sounded like a character from a spy movie.

Mallory followed him into an office at the end of the hall. The office, with its view of a parking lot, was filled with papers and equipment for viewing digital films. There were stacks of scripts on a shelf, and a couple of shirts and a jacket tossed over a chair. A Chinese food container had been left on a small table. Jason Blackthorne was sexy as sin, but his office was a mess.

He perched on the only free spot at the edge of his desk and gestured her into a chair.

Mallory's belly felt tight, and she was aware that her palm was damp from holding the binder. But she plastered on a smile, remembered all she'd learned from YouTube tutorial *Putting Your Best Foot Forward: Strategies for Job Interviews*, and said, "Thank you for seeing me today. I just want to say, I am a perfect match for this opportunity."

"Oh," he said.

She sat a little straighter. "May I tell you how?"

"Sure," he said, and folded his arms across his middle.

Mallory began to talk. She was aware of how hazel green his eyes were, how thick his hair. He was wearing a hoodie over a T-shirt and jeans, and Jordans on his feet. He had an air of casual sophistication, which, for the first time in her life, Mallory got.

He was terribly distracting as she rattled off her qualifications for the job.

He said nothing as she talked. He asked no questions. From time to time, his gaze strayed to her binder. When she reached the part of her talk that drew from past series such as *Columbo* and *Cagney and Lacey* one of his dark brows arched with surprise. "You know a lot about detective dramas."

She knew a lot about television. "It's a niche interest," she admitted.

When she had finished, he sighed, as if she had worn him out. Entirely possible. Mallory had a tendency to thoroughness. Which she'd pointed out to him, as well as being a self-starter, goal-oriented, and dedicated to her craft.

"What's in the binder?" he asked.

"Letters of recommendation and my transcripts, and some story boards from some short films I've made, in case you have questions."

He looked at the binder. He looked out the window. He asked what she would do differently in his office, and she said she didn't know, that she'd need a few days to study workflow. He smirked and said something about there being no workflow, only chaos, and then asked, "Do you have an iPhone?"

Odd question. "Yes."

"Do you know how to use the *Find my Phone*?"

"Ah…sure."

"Good. I lose my phone a lot. Do you think you could keep that stocked?" He pointed at a small fridge.

Mallory looked long and hard at that fridge. "I, ah…" What was this? The job had said an assistant to the showrunner.

"I have low blood sugar," he said.

"Oh. Sure, I could do that." She could do it with her eyes closed. She had done it for her entire family since she was twelve.

"Great." He glanced at his watch. "I'm a little disorganized, so I need help with that."

Totally obvious, judging by the mess in his office. "Sure," she said.

He pushed away from his desk, and he looked at her again, but this time, his gaze held hers a little longer than was entirely necessary, and he said, "Can you start Monday?"

"What?"

"I think you met Holly on her way out," he said. "I need someone right away."

"Oh." Mallory stood up and tried to keep the grin from her face. "Yes! Eight a.m.?"

He chuckled. "Don't go crazy. Let's say nine."

She smiled. She stuck out her hand. "Thank you."

He took her hand and she gripped it. "Should I check in with Human Resources?"

"Ah…you can check in Monday."

She let go his hand. Neither of them spoke for a moment, just looked at each other. A smile lit his face, and damn it if that smile didn't trickle through her like a slow moving stream. Just spreading warmth all the way down to the tips of her toes. "Monday," he said, and pointed at her.

"Monday," she said, and pointed back like a dolt. She gathered her things and went out the door, her face beaming.

She was halfway home when she remembered she hadn't asked him how much the job paid. Oh well. Anything was better than nothing at this point.

———

Inez was in the kitchen when Mallory came home, clad in a bathrobe and her head wrapped in a towel. "Hey!" Mallory said brightly.

"That's my dress," Inez responded. "And my shoes!"

"We're going to dinner to celebrate my new job!"

Inez eyed her curiously. "You got a job? How are we going to dinner? I thought you were broke. Also, you really don't have to do my laundry and fold it and put it away, Mallory. And did you really organize my closet by color? Because I am pretty sure that didn't happen by accident."

"I got a job! And I am *so* broke. But I'm confident that's about to change," she'd said with a wink and all the optimism of a genie in a bottle. "For the record, I don't mind doing your laundry. It's something to do. Also, I felt like your closet was a pressing need that definitely should be addressed, so I addressed it. I can be ready in ten."

"What about my dress?" Inez shouted after her. Mallory laughed.

They went to a nearby Mexican restaurant they frequented. Mallory ordered margaritas and filled Inez in on the details of her job. "It's the executive assistant to the CEO of a production company. But he also happens to be the executive producer *and* the showrunner for a project that was just greenlit by Netflix. It's perfect! It is exactly in line with my goals. *All* my goals."

"What's the show?" Inez asked curiously. "Film? Series? Documentary?"

"A series. I checked it out—it's already gotten a lot of buzz in the trades. It's a gritty detective drama that explores the dark side of humanity," Mallory intoned with the dramatic flare of a program announcer. "It's called *Bad Intentions*."

That's when fortune's smile dimmed. Inez looked up. Her big brown eyes narrowed into near slits. "Did you just say *Bad Intentions*?"

"Yep. I said those exact words. *Bad Intentions*."

Inez wrinkled her nose and stabbed some lettuce onto her fork. "Is the CEO named Jason by any chance?"

"What? Why?"

Inez looked at her.

"Yes. His name is Jason with Blackthorne Entertainment. How did you know that?"

Inez shook her head and stabbed more lettuce. "You don't want that job, Mallory."

Well *that* wasn't true—Mallory wanted this job like she wanted to breathe. "Yes, I do."

"You don't."

Mallory put her fork down and sat back, staring at her friend. "I really *do* want this job. I want it so bad I'm about to pop."

"Please don't pop in my dress."

"What exactly is the problem, Inez? This is what I've been looking for. It's an opportunity to learn about every aspect of making a show. I am so lucky to have stumbled into a job with a company that actually has some irons in the fire. It's kismet. It's like I'm in class and going to lab and learning how to do everything. So yeah, if you ask me, this job is pretty perfect." She picked up her margarita to toast Inez's margarita, but Inez didn't budge, so Mallory reached across the table and clinked glasses on her own. "Come on, Nezzy!

Be happy for me! I have experience. I have film credits, I have directing credits—"

Inez pointed her fork at Mallory's nose. "First, don't call me Nezzy. My brothers used to call me Nezzy when they were terrorizing me. Second, you do *not* have directing credits. Seriously, Mallory, you can't claim directing credits from YouTube short films that you posted to an audience of like, what, fifteen views?"

It was more like twenty-five views, but Mallory wasn't going to argue. It really only came down to a matter of the right marketing. "Never mind that. I am very interested in this job. I've been working in this industry for ten years and I'm very good at what I do."

One of Inez's dark brows rose up with skepticism.

"Okay, not the acting part," Mallory amended with a dismissive flick of her wrist, although she still didn't believe she was *that* bad. She thought back to some of her more iconic roles—Girl No. 2 on the subway. Bar customer. It was different for Inez. She had sleek black hair and soulful brown eyes and a lot of talent. Whereas one casting director had told Mallory that no one wanted an actress with short blonde hair, and to lose ten. "But I *am* good behind the scenes," she insisted. "And I want to direct. I am a *good* director. I know how to tell a story and all I need is a break. So why shouldn't I go for it? I did some research on this show. Netflix is putting some money behind it. They started filming the first season last month. See how perfect it is?"

Inez put down her fork. She pushed her plate away, folded her arms in front of her, tossed her dark hair over her shoulder in the same manner that had won her the role as the office receptionist in a major motion picture starring Ryan Reynolds and Rebel Wilson. "I'm going to explain to you why it's *not* perfect, and don't argue. The CEO of Blackthorne Entertainment is Jason Blackthorne. And he's notorious."

Mallory gasped. "He's a predator?"

"No!" Inez scoffed. "Well, I don't know, maybe he is. I don't know about that. I mean he's notorious for going through assistants like you go through chocolate."

Mallory was slightly offended, but honestly, she could motor through some chocolate. "That's just Hollywood. Everyone is hard to work for," she tried, but Inez was already shaking her head.

"He has a bad rep, okay? He's one of those workaholics you hear about—all day and all night and expects his assistant to do the same. He drives them into the ground and then, of course, he gets all the credit."

If that's all it was, Mallory could handle it. She'd survived two "hippie parents" who were really neither hippies nor parents. "Not scared," she said pertly. "I can pour myself into a job with the best of them. What else you got?"

"I heard this story of him sending an assistant to Canada to get a certain brand of flannel jackets for a scene. Not just any flannel would do."

Mallory shrugged. She understood that, actually. When one was creating art, one could not use inferior materials.

"In the middle of winter."

"So sue him for the inconvenience."

"A snow storm blew in while the assistant was shopping for the jacket that could have been shipped, mind you, but Jason Blackthorne wanted it first thing in the morning. The assistant's flight was grounded."

"Okay. *Super* inconvenient."

"It was three days before he could get back. His plants died. His dog didn't recognize him. They'd declared him dead and rented out his apartment, and he got post-traumatic stress, and then, Jason Blackthorne fired him."

"Yeah, okay," Mallory said, scowling. "I see what you're doing."

"I'm just saying," Inez said, and picked up her fork. "There's something else, too."

"Let me guess—he hates babies. He kicked a cat."

"No. He's super good-looking."

Mallory perked up. "You have no idea."

"Oh, I've seen him. And I know how you get."

"How I *get*?"

"Yes. You turn into a spineless doormat when you're attracted to handsome men and organize the shit out of their lives. It's bad enough you do *my* laundry."

"That is ridiculous," she scoffed. "And you're mixing your metaphors."

"Sam Harris." Inez punctuated that by stuffing an enormous bite into her mouth.

"That was different," Mallory said. "He was very good at making me believe he liked the things I did for him."

"Carlos."

"Carlos is your cousin! I didn't do anything for him."

"He said you were ironing his T-shirts."

Mallory sensed the theme. "I wasn't doing it on a regular basis, I did it *once*. Because they were ridiculously wrinkled." She leaned forward and said low, "He *never* takes his clothes out of the drier. He actually pulls clothes from the drier and wears them."

"Don't tell me," Inez said. "But you are the only one who started doing his laundry. You do everything for everyone, and then you're, like, *super* helpful if they're hot, and you end up getting used, Mallory."

"For the record, it is really hard to date someone in wrinkled shirts. Instant turn off. But here is the difference. I am not planning on dating Jason Blackthorne. I'm not even going to look at him. I will not be doing his laundry."

"Sure. I'm just saying, he's the kind of guy to run right over a woman, and you're the kind of woman to be run over, especially if he's hot."

That might have been insulting to hear from anyone else, but Mallory could not deny there was some truth to it. She held out her hand. "If I regret even a moment of it, you have my permission to say I told you so. Pinky swear."

Inez wasted no time in taking advantage of that swear with her pinky.

Mallory clasped her hands together in prayer pose and bowed her head. And then she speared a tomato from Inez's plate.

"I'm going to go ahead and get a jump-start on this," Inez said, picking up her fork. "I told you so."

In the weeks and months that followed, Inez never missed an opportunity to tell Mallory *I told you so.* And she didn't just say it, she gloated. She laughed roundly when Mallory complained about Jason, which Mallory did a lot, usually spurred on with lots of wine.

Because Inez was right—Jason Blackthorne was hell on wheels. He was demanding, he was disorganized, he had no respect for Mallory's time, he asked what she thought then dismissed her opinion. He wanted the impossible and never seemed to fully appreciate when the impossible was accomplished.

That was enough to make her almost hate him. He could be insufferable, even when Mallory could see his vision and how important this show was to him. He'd said more than once he had a lot riding on it. He was a driven man.

But Inez was right about something else—he was a very handsome man. He smelled like honey and lemon and something else that was entirely masculine and could rev up Mallory's mojo like she was on steroids. Couple that with his great ideas, and the passion he had for filming stories that matched her own, and Mallory had developed a not insignificant crush on him. And she wasn't entirely sure he hadn't developed one on her. She was probably imagining things, but it seemed like every time they were in a room together, the air sizzled. And there was the time she was copying a script, and he'd had to squeeze by, and he'd squeegeed his package across her ass. He apologized profusely, but the way he looked at her and she looked at him was pretty thrilling. And that was just the tip of the iceberg.

Inez loved to remind her, "You just can't pull yourself away from all that luscious, beautiful man, can you? *Told* you."

"Not true," Mallory would insist. "I'm waiting for a chance to kill him. It has to be the right moment so I don't get caught."

That was somewhat true. She was learning so much about how to put a show together. It was invaluable experience that was translating into her own work. And the more she learned, the more ideas she had. She kept a running list, and when she caught Jason alone for a moment, she'd spring into action, suggesting ways to streamline production, ideas for scenes, her thoughts on character development. She believed if she could convince Jason to give her a shot at directing, he would see just how in sync they were about the vision for this series and perhaps even other projects.

Unfortunately, Jason tended to take her suggestions and

sort of nod them away. "*Great idea, Mallory. Is there any yogurt in the office fridge? Could you run out and get some?*"

She was often confused by how one minute she wanted to punch him in the face and in the next breath want to kiss him. Like all over his ridiculously fit body. Not that she would *ever*. He was her boss, and he was impossible, and it would be playing with fire.

Oh, that fire. It was a glowing ember in her. Sometimes, she would catch him looking at her in a way that made her feel a little weak in the knees. Once, after a particularly difficult episode with a lot of stunts ended without injury or cost overrun, they had shared a look that had been almost orgasmic. It was obvious, they both loved this gig.

When she came into work, his gaze would flick over her, and he'd say something like, "Nice dress. Did you have to hire someone to paint it on?" And she would say, "No. But I'll be looking for volunteers to scrape it off." His eyes would go dark, and run down her body, and then he'd turn back to his work and she would run to the ladies' room and grip the edge of the sink and chastise herself in the mirror. "What are you *doing*?"

There were little touches here and there, too, more than was necessary. It was like the day at the copy machine, but much more subtle. Their fingers would tangle when she handed him a paper. He'd bring something to her desk and put his hand on her shoulder to lean over her.

She had the full Monty of all crushes on him, and she hated that she did, because she had learned so much, her short films were beginning to get some traction in contests and on YouTube.

And then one night, Mallory set the embers on fire, and the fire spread.

She and Jason had been working late, watching the rough

cuts from that day's shooting and, because it was late, there was wine involved. Jason was teasing her. He admired how she had arranged the Post-its on his whiteboard so it was clear what changes had to be made to what scenes, and then commented that the motivational posters she'd put up around the room had finally motivated him.

She was laughing about something one of the crew had said, in an unguarded, unprofessional moment, Jason said, "Has anyone ever told you how sexy you are in a totally uptight prosecutor kind of way?"

Funny how ridiculously pleased Mallory had been made by the compliment. She'd said, "Has anyone ever told you how sexy you are in a totally demanding asshole kind of way?"

Jason had leaned back, smiling at her. "I think that is the most honest thing anyone has ever said to me." He grinned, and he tapped her knee with his fist. "If I didn't know better, I'd think you were flirting with me, Mallory Price."

She was on the verge of admitting it, but Jason laughed, and his sparkly, Christmas light smile had shot into her, and he said, "Kidding."

"I have a major crush on you," Mallory blurted. The words just tumbled out of her mouth. They just fell, right there between them, and at the time, Mallory didn't care. She was smiling, she felt light and buzzy and they were at a boring part of the dailies that she absolutely would cut as it didn't advance the plot of this particular episode one iota if anyone would listen to her.

"What?" Jason had asked uncertainly. He'd sat up, both feet on the ground, his hands clasped between his knees.

"Should I not have told you? I mean, didn't you guess?"

"I think," he said slowly, "that you were the one who reminded me, in the middle of that issue with the craft services, that the Human Resources manual strictly forbid workplace fraternization."

"Yes, that was me. I thought you needed to know." She was looking at his mouth and thinking what an odd word fraternization was. "Is fraternizing the same as flirting? I was trying to flirt," she said, pressing a hand to her heart. "I think technically, they are two different things."

"I wouldn't know," Jason said as his gaze was drifting down her body. "I leave that sort of thing to you. I assume since you are so by the book, you know what you're talking about. What is the proper response when someone in the workplace is flirting with you?"

Well, she hadn't memorized the Human Resource manual, for God's sake, and downed the rest of her wine and tossed—or dropped—the glass aside. She inched her way to the end of her chair. She could remember how alive she'd felt in that moment, because Jason was looking at her like she was chocolate cake buried in ice cream. "I think you should turn a blind eye." And then, the spirit moved her. Moved her all the way over to his chair. She brazenly straddled Jason, like she was the star of her own little movie and did things like this (she did not) and he let her, his hands landing on her hips, a light shining somewhere deep into his deliciously hazel eyes.

"Miss Price, I really like your initiative."

"You know what I like? Your mouth," Mallory said in the sultriest voice she could manage, and touched her lips to his.

"That is so *weird*," Jason said. "Because I like yours, too." He kissed her back, but in a much better way than she had kissed him. His hands found their way under her blouse and began a slow slide up her rib cage to cup her breast as his tongue slipped into her mouth.

She could taste him, taste the wine. She'd felt a sparkle erupting in her and spreading quickly, shimmering down her veins. It was pure brilliance shining between them. She was straddling him like she knew what she was doing, and he was getting hard, and he was the best kisser in the world, and she was melting inside, her body melting from all the sparkling and want, and she wanted desperately for him to slide right on inside her.

Maybe Jason wanted it, too, because he suddenly stood up *with* her, which she would not have thought possible, and sat her on the conference table. He caught her chin in his hand and held her head still so he could really kiss her. Kiss her so deeply and so thoroughly as shocks of pleasure waved through her. Mallory had no choice but to grab on to him before she melted onto the floor. If she'd known that kissing him would be this electric, she would have found an excuse to kiss him a long time ago.

Jason stepped in between her legs, and her pencil skirt rode up to her hips, exposing her red lacy thong panties to him. "*Jesus*," he said. "Mallory, this is…very unexpected," he said again, and had begun to kiss her all over again.

Mallory could look back on that kiss now and easily say it was the most exciting kiss she'd ever experienced. Maybe because it was technically forbidden by standard workplace decorum. Maybe because she never thought a man as handsome and accomplished as Jason Blackthorne would be interested in her. And she had no doubt she could have had it all, but then…*but then*…

Her damn conscience had pierced the fizzy pleasure and had reminded her that Jason was her *boss*, and she needed this job if she was ever going to get a leg up in this industry, and it was so clichéd to be doing it through sex. So in spite of feeling incredibly sexy, and the certainty that it could have been one of the best nights of her life, Mallory slid off the table and out from underneath his touch.

The next day, of course, she'd been completely mortified by her behavior. She had wanted to say something about it, to address the ten-ton elephant in the room. But she never did. In fact, neither of them ever mentioned it. They simply carried on with that crackle and sizzle following them around and casting tension between every look, every touch.

In other words, Mallory had been playing with fire ever since that night.

But she was *not* doing his laundry.

CHAPTER TWO

In the beginning, Jason had to pinch himself that, at long last, he was really running a production company and producing a television show. Against the odds, he'd gotten his shot.

It had been a long time coming—a lot of hard work, a lot of jobs on productions that had gone nowhere. A lot of begging and pushing back when doors had closed.

But it had paid off and it was definitely happening. The first three episodes of *Bad Intentions* had been distributed to critics. The first episode had aired to reviews that were good for the most part. He was pleased and relieved that his vision for a series around a detective that skirted on the edge of the law and life was not rejected out of hand.

The pre-production phase for season two was done, and production would begin in about ten days for the second season. The first season had been shot in a studio in Culver City, but the lease was expensive and Jason and the crew felt it lacked atmosphere. So the second season would include scenes shot in King Harbor, the summer home of the Black-thornes for decades.

Jason had come last week with his Director of Photography, Neil Tarelli; the production designer, Maleeka Johnson, who developed the visual style of the series; and Cass Farenthold, the director. Together, they had scouted location. But Cass being Cass—difficult, in other words,—had, at the last minute, changed his mind. It was bothersome—the cast and crew were on hiatus until production began in earnest. And maybe it was Jason's imagination, but Cass seemed more difficult than normal. Like he was picking arguments for the sake of arguing.

In the end, it was decided that Neil and Maleeka would return to L.A. and their hiatus, and Jason and Cass would stay and work out the last couple of locations.

Jason had invited Cass to stay at the family compound, but Cass had refused. "I do most of my work at night," he'd said. Whatever that meant.

In spite of Cass's perennial displeasure with everything and everyone, all was going great. So great, in fact, that Jason should have known a shoe would drop. More like a steel-toed work boot, and right on his head.

At the Blackthorne family estate in King Harbor, Jason laced up his tennis shoes for a run. It was so early that the sun was still a slender pink line on the edge of the ocean. Ross would say Jason was crazy, running this early, and maybe he was. But he needed to sweat off some energy. He hadn't slept well last night. He really hadn't slept at all—he'd received some significantly bad news late afternoon yesterday.

He ran down the path, away from the house, to the shore. There was a path that followed the coastline around, up on to a promontory, and down again. About two miles out, he'd come into King Harbor, where he'd turn around and run two miles back to the estate. He would need all four miles to pound out the anxiety and anger that had flowed in his veins all night.

It was maddening that shit like this kept happening, but Darien Simmons, the star of his show, a veteran actor with several Emmys and a few Tonys under his belt, and for whom Jason had paid an exorbitant sum because he needed that kind of talent, had been credibly accused of sexual assault by a production intern on the show. *His* show. An eighteen-year-old intern at that. Darien was the same age as Jason's uncle Graham. Why were men such dicks? And how was it that some men could force themselves on women who didn't want it? Jason didn't get it. If the feelings weren't patently mutual, he was never interested.

When Jason had called Darien in Vegas, Darien said, perhaps predictably, that the young woman had started it. And perhaps just as predictably, the young woman and Gloria Allred, the famous attorney inclined to take on cases like this, said Darien cornered her and stuck his tongue down her throat and shoved his hand up her skirt. Charming.

Jason fired him. Cass had accused him of responding in a knee-jerk fashion, but Jason didn't think so. There was no room for that behavior on his show. None. Cass was beside himself. He said Jason was responsible for the shit show they were about to film.

The news did not get better from there. Netflix was already questioning Jason's decision to film on location in Maine. The brass there was not happy when he called them to let them know about Darien.

He paused running up the hill to catch his breath and looked back at his family's summer home. He'd come back to Maine because he'd grown up here. This is where he'd turned to movies when his parents had died in a plane crash when he was twelve years old. This is where he and his brothers and cousins had made themselves a family. It seemed natural to come back here.

The studio didn't like the idea at all. It would cost too much, they said. But Jason convinced them that it was the right thing to do. King Harbor was perfect. It was beautiful here, there was no question. But with the right filters and lighting, with the right locations, it could also look like a dark, scary place. Jason could trade on his name here, use it to access places that might otherwise be inaccessible.

In their tour of places around town, Neil and Maleeka had agreed with Jason on the places they'd found for filming specific scenes. Only Cass had disagreed. He had wanted to use the Vault, a pub attached to the whisky distillery his family owned. But the Vault didn't seem right to the rest of them. For Jason, because it was too attached to his family. They hung out there when they were in town, and it seemed too upscale for the series. They had talked Cass out of the Vault, but he was digging his heels in at every turn, and Jason had begun to wonder why. There was no team player in that man.

But right now, his biggest problem was Darien Simmons. Or rather, the sudden absence of Darien Simmons, damn him. The whole thing baffled him. He didn't get that kind of lust. He much preferred women who were equal. Who had lived a little, who knew their own minds. He was attracted to women who gave as good as they got. And if she didn't, he quickly grew bored. His history of dating fame seekers and actress wannabes had left him currently unattached. It seemed like he never found women he was attracted to who were attracted to him, exactly. They were more attracted to what he could do for them. Maybe he was just going about it all wrong. He didn't really know—he was always in the throes of a project, trying to get something off the ground, and never had time to think about it.

With the exception of Mallory. Now, there was a woman who could give as good as she got, plus organize your shooting schedule while she was at it. He didn't know if she was certified OCD or what, but her ability to organize down to the last paperclip kept production humming along like a fine machine. He didn't know how he would have managed this long without her. He also didn't know how he'd gone this far in his life without knowing he loved the smell of jasmine until he'd detected it on her.

Mallory was going to flip out when she heard the news about Darien. Because Mallory was also a little straightlaced. He was pretty sure she would not abide lapses in moral character.

Jason's first thought was that he'd have to fly back to L.A. to work through this debacle. But the more he thought about it, he decided that was not a great idea. There was too much to do in King Harbor to get the production up and going, and any delay would only draw attention to the role Darien had had here. Not to mention the increase to production costs. So he'd spent the better part of last night on the phone with publicity and lawyers and Netflix, trying to keep a lid on this boiling pot. Darien was looking for some air cover. Jason was not going to be the one to give it to him. Netflix was drafting a statement today announcing the severing of their relationship with Darien Simmons.

And now Jason had a casting crisis.

He started running again. He had to get someone on board as quickly as possible and he was going to need help. Which meant Mallory was going to have to come to Maine—it was the most expedient solution. She could work here for a few days until the focus on Darien's behavior moved away from *Bad Intentions*, and they had a new star attached.

He suddenly stopped running and looked at the ocean below him. The thin line of pink on the horizon had turned gold. The sun was about to appear. He dug his phone from his pocket and called Mallory.

Mallory definitely wasn't thinking about how sexy Jason was when she was jolted out of a dead sleep by the insistent foghorn ringtone she'd assigned to him. It disoriented her—it was dark, and she wasn't sure where her phone was, or where *she* was for that matter, and fumbled around for it while she tried to focus.

She was exhausted. With Jason on location in Maine, and the cast and crew on hiatus, Mallory had been completely engrossed in making her latest short film. Meaning, when she wasn't relaying Jason's instructions to someone else on hiatus, generally barked out at her because he was always in a hurry, she was filming.

The man could not seem to put down his phone. It was all incredibly stressful, particularly because no one in Hollywood saw her as anything more than Jason's mouthpiece. She had no authority.

It was very annoying to technically be on vacation and have one's boss always calling, which she had pointed out to Jason.

"I see your point," he said. "I'll pay you double time this week."

Well of course that had made her perk up, but still. It was the principle of the thing. And she really wanted to focus on her new short film. A small new film company, Morning

Moonlight, had seen her last entry in a dramatic short film contest, and had brought her in for an interview. A few days later, they had extended her an offer to join their team.

Mallory was thrilled. She told them she needed a couple of weeks to think about it, but really what she wanted was to finish her current project and show that to them, too. She had lined up an ex-boyfriend to do the camera work and Inez and another mutual friend were the cast. She had only three more scenes to shoot, and the plan was to get them shot before Jason came back. Because when he came back, he'd be crazed with the production of season two and would not leave her alone—she'd learned that the hard way through season one production. Jason thought nothing of calling her at all hours during the production, and in anticipation of that, Mallory had had to cajole her friends into shooting all week, sometimes into the night.

The phone stopped ringing. *Thank God.*

Mallory fumbled around for her glasses and looked at the clock. It was three thirty in the morning. *Three thirty in the God bless morning.* She rolled onto her back and heard a crackling. She reached beneath her and pulled out a bag of potato chips. Oh right—she'd been stuffing them in out of sheer hunger because she hadn't had time for dinner. Apparently, she'd fallen asleep with them.

Where was her phone, anyway?

She swept her hand over her bed. Something under the sheet jabbed her hand. She groped for the offending thing and pulled out her notebook. The spiral end had snagged her. Mallory remembered now—she'd fallen asleep watching an episode of *Bad Intentions* and making notes.

The first season had just started airing. *Variety* said it was an intriguing update to the standard crime drama. *Vulture* said it was gritty noir, but offered nothing new. It had a 90 percent rating on *Rotten Tomatoes*. It was a *good* show, there was no doubt. But Mallory thought it could be even better. She thought it could be groundbreaking. She had studied all the detective dramas she could get her hands on and she knew what Jason had developed with this one could be so good. So she'd been watching the episodes, making meticulous notes about things she would have done differently had she directed them. Her plan was to get a few minutes of Jason's time when he came back to present her ideas. Her goal was to get him to agree to let her direct at least a couple of scenes this season.

All of this was easier said than done. The director, Mr. Cass Farenthold of feature film fame and two Oscar nominations under his belt, did not appreciate feedback. He walked around the set as if he was doing them all a favor by showing up. But from Mallory's vantage point, he didn't care enough about *Bad Intentions*. During the filming of the last couple of episodes of season one, she'd felt like the series was doing well because of the dedication of the veteran actors, but that Cass was phoning it in. She suspected she knew why, too. An assistant to an executive at Sony Pictures had told her over drinks one night that Sony and Cass had been in discussions for a first look deal, but that Cass had a contract issue with Jason. Meaning, he had to be released from his contract with Jason to pursue the other deal.

She tossed the notebook onto the floor and closed her eyes, drifting back to sleep. But her heart suffered another painful start when her phone began to ring again. She really had to change that ringtone. She spread her hands around her bed, looking for the phone, and found it under a pillow.

"Hello?" she croaked.

"Mallory!" Jason said. He sounded breathless, like he was panicked.

"What? Oh my God has something *happened*? Is it your parents? Did something happen to your parents?"

"My parents? Why would you say that? My parents are dead, Mallory," Jason said in a voice that was far too calm to relay such news at this late hour.

"Oh my God! *How*?"

"A plane crash when I was twelve," he said matter-of-factly. "You don't know that?"

How would she know that? It's not like they sat around the break room talking about their childhoods. "Then what has happened?"

"Everyone is fine," he said. "Why are you so hoarse?"

She was going to kill him. "It's three thirty in the morning, Jason, that's why. Who calls at this time in the morning? You scared the crap out of me!"

"Three thirty in the—oh, man, sorry, Mallory," Jason said jovially. "Brain freeze. I forgot you were on the West Coast. I've been so caught up in things going on here."

He *forgot*? He could be so insensitive at times. "Well it is, and if you don't mind, I'm going back to sleep."

"I didn't think," he said, talking over her. "I'm out for a run. *Beautiful* morning here."

"I'm so happy that you're enjoying it," she snapped. "I was enjoying my sleep."

"Just makes you feel alive," he continued, as if he couldn't hear her. "You know, I grew up here, but I forget how great…"

She didn't hear what else he said. She had to yawn. And then she sneezed. She rubbed her nose. "Jason," she tried.

"Did you get that?" he asked.

Was he still talking? She was *so tired*. "Get what?" she asked through another yawn.

"I need you to come to Maine."

Mallory blinked. She snorted. "For a moment there, I thought you said I should come to Maine."

"I did say that. You really, like, need to get a cup of coffee or something, Mal. You sound like a truck driver who hasn't slept in a few days."

"I *haven't* slept, Jason. I've been super busy." She pushed herself up to sitting. All she could think about in that moment was her short film. She was so close to being done. "I can't come to Maine."

"Why not? Look, it's not a big deal. You fly out as soon as you can, you're back in a couple of days."

"No!" Mallory insisted, and got out of bed. She didn't know where she was headed, she just felt the need to be standing. "You can't call me at three thirty in the morning and tell me to get on a plane if there isn't an emerg— *Ouch!* Crap! I think I broke my toe."

"Better watch where you're going."

"I really, really want to kick you right now," she said. "It's *dark*."

"So what's the problem with coming to Maine for a couple of days?" he asked, glossing over the possibility of a broken toe. "Three, max."

Mallory groaned. Her toe, it seemed, was not broken. Just as annoyed as she was. "But *why*? There is so much to do here."

"Here's why, Mallory. Keep this on the down-low, but we have a crisis brewing. Darien has been accused of sexual assault with one of the production interns. It will hit the news tomorrow."

"*What?*" Mallory shouted, shocked. "Oh my God! Oh my *God*." Darien Simmons was a well-regarded actor. He was tall and stately and charming and the gray around the temples made him sexy. Mallory was shocked, but maybe she shouldn't be—this seemed to keep happening in this town. "Who? What did he say?"

"Some eighteen-year-old intern is all I know. He said there was no truth to it. That she came on to him."

Mallory snorted her opinion of that.

"I fired him."

Mallory gasped. "You *fired* him?"

"In a minute," Jason said emphatically. "Forget the kind of attention it's going to bring the show, which, let me tell you, no one is going to like, and *everyone*, from our investors on down to the grip, are going to have an opinion about, but personally, I have a real issue with men assaulting women and I don't want it anywhere near my show. We need to replace him and fast. The casting director is putting together some headshots. I'm going to have to make a quick decision."

Mallory was still absorbing the news that Darien had been fired. That he'd abused a production intern, probably some girl who had stars in her eyes and was hoping to get a foot in the door. "But what…how—"

"See? Lots of questions. And I have a lot of phone calls to make. I need you to come, Mallory. Hire a plane."

"No! Wait, Jason, let me think. We can't just hire a plane—"

"I'll find room in the budget."

"It's not that." There was plenty of money in the budget for emergencies, she'd made sure of it. "It's the emissions! We've *talked* about this—"

"Okay, you can get the middle seat in coach on a commercial flight, although I don't see how that fixes the emissions problem or whatever it is you're worried about. Is that what you want me to do?"

Mallory squeezed her eyes shut. "That's hardly a choice."

"I'll call my guy and send a plane. Be ready to go in about, oh, I don't know, about six hours."

"Jason!" She shoved her fingers through her hair trying to think. "I have plans. That's the other thing we talked about, remember? That you can't just assume I'm available at all hours of the day and night."

"I will make sure you're well compensated for this, Mallory. I'll let you write your own check."

She rolled her eyes. "It doesn't actually work that way. It *never* works that way."

"I'll make it up to you. It's just a few days, not a lifestyle change. So pull on those sweatpants you like for weekend work hours and be ready to go."

Sweatpants! "It's called athleisure wear and it's really in right now—"

He was panting again. He was talking and running, she realized. That was so like Jason, doing fourteen things at once. "You'll be flying into King Harbor, Maine. Text me when you book the plane and let me know when you're taking off. I'll have someone to pick you up."

"I thought you said you were going to call your guy."

"It's easier if I text you his name and you book it. Actually, book a ride while you're at it. King Harbor Limos."

"I don't—how am I supposed to…" She shook her head. "This is the worst thing you've ever done to me, Jason."

"The worst?" He laughed. "Think of it as an adventure! Okay, so I really have to go. Text me and let me know what the plans are."

Mallory hated him in that dark, middle-of-the-night moment. She was going to quit this stupid job and take the one at Morning Moonlight and he could find someone else to find his stupid phone.

"You can't quit," he said, as if he was reading her mind.

"Are you still there?" she demanded, a little surprised he hadn't hung up.

"Remember the contract you signed? You have to give me at least two weeks' notice. So listen, it's a six-hour flight. You can do some work on the plane if you need to."

"Wow, thank you," she said.

"Or, you can sleep on the plane. Whatever, just get here. I really have to go, Mal. We're in for a real shit storm today. See you soon." The line went dead.

Mallory tossed the phone on the bed. She covered her face with her hands. She could hear Inez's voice in her head. "*He can't keep anyone.*"

Yeah, well, this was why. But she didn't have the time or the energy to examine it right now. She had to get ready to fly to Maine where she couldn't promise herself that she wouldn't punch Jason right in the kisser.

Damn Jason Blackthorne. Damn him for being so ridiculously handsome, for being so ridiculously demanding. Damn him for lighting that fire because she was actually going to get on that plane.

But this time, she wasn't going to let his demand just go, swept up under the rug of more demands and impossible expectations. She didn't know how just yet, but she thought now would be a good time to tell him about that other job offer.

Darien Simmons. *Really?*

CHAPTER THREE

JASON FELT BAD ABOUT WAKING MALLORY UP. SOMETIMES, he was so in his own head that he forgot things that were pretty important. Like time zones. Mallory was the one who always remembered things like time zones. Mallory remembered everything. She never made mistakes like that and she made damn sure he didn't, either.

He looked at the ocean again. The sun was casting gold across the surface. For Jason, this was the best part of the day, before people began moving and the earth began turning and phones began pinging and emails began flooding his inbox. This was the time of day he cleared his mind and made sense of the millions of thoughts that pinged around his head. A television production was extremely hard work. He could not have guessed how hard until he'd done it. He'd imagined it, dreamed of it, but until he was actually at the helm of the trenches, he couldn't conceive it.

Before the crisis with Darien, he'd been thinking about the first two scripts for season two of *Bad Intentions*. It was early yet, and the reviews were just beginning to come in for the first season, and yes, they were good, but Jason had seen a

review in *The Atlantic* for the first episode, and it wasn't
good. What had it said? Something like, *Bad Intentions, the
creation of Executive Producer Jason Blackthorne, and
highly decorated director Cass Farenthold, misses the mark.
What could have been a unique idea in a crowded field of
crime dramas is hampered by an execution that is leaden and
contrived. The stellar cast saves it from disaster.*

Jason knew better than to let reviews sink into his psyche.
But the thing was, he'd had a similar reaction when he'd
watched the first episode on television at a viewing party with
some of the cast and crew. It had been a few months since
he'd seen the final edited version, and he had to admit, with
that time and distance, he noticed the heavy hand with the
camera angles, the clunky transitions, the bad lighting. Neil
had fired the gaffer after the first episode aired. He'd brought
in a new guy who was twice as expensive. "You gotta have
the right kind of lighting," he'd assured Jason, but Jason still
worried.

Cass said he didn't see what the concern was. He'd
remarked as much as he'd tucked into an enormous slab of
beef. "Looks good to me," he'd said with a dismissive shrug.

The funny thing was, Mallory had mentioned the lighting
when they were filming. Jason could clearly remember it, her
standing beside him with her ever-present binder and mutter-
ing, "This is not going to look right on the small screen."

Jason had ignored her comment. He had the best in the
industry, and Mallory was his assistant. She didn't know a
fraction of what those men knew. She'd said it again during
editing, and again he hadn't listened. Neither had Neil. "The
gaffer knows what he is doing," he'd assured Jason.

Funny how no one seemed to remember that now.
Mallory was right. And yet, she never threw it back at him. In
fact, she'd been very encouraging when he'd mentioned the

review in *The Atlantic*. "You're missing the bigger picture," she'd said. And then she'd had their publicity department pull together several reviews to demonstrate that most were good and did not mention poor lighting. "Story is the thing," she'd said. "That's what has to be on point. You can have the best production values in the world, but if you don't have a good story, you lose."

He had discovered that she could be surprisingly astute about this crazy industry sometimes, especially for an assistant with no experience. Jason knew he was being paranoid about the reviews, but no one in his industry or his company understood what a big deal this Netflix production was for him.

It was everything.

First, he'd had to borrow money from the family coffers to get his entertainment company off the ground. There had been conditions to that—his entertainment company had to be branded as part of the Blackthorne suite of businesses. And Blackthornes didn't put their name on just anything, as he'd been reminded over and over again all his life.

The Blackthorne brand had begun more than one hundred years ago when his great grandparents emigrated from Scotland, bringing their secret to distilling good whisky with them. Over the next one hundred years, the Blackthorne brand had become synonymous with excellence. No one made better whisky than the Blackthorne distillery. No one in the world, to hear his family tell it.

Jason's uncle Graham, his brother Brock, and his cousin, Trey, had been hard on Jason when he'd come to Blackthorne Enterprises to ask them to invest in his production company so he could get it off the ground. It wasn't a surprise to anyone he was asking—Jason had been pursuing this avenue of life for years. And yet, he got the lecture. He would never forget that day, the way he'd stared out the window of the Blackthorne Enterprise offices in the Hancock Tower in Boston, at the sweeping views of Back Bay, the Charles River, and Boston Harbor. "The Blackthornes don't put their name on just anything, Jason. If you see the name Blackthorne, you expect excellent quality."

"This isn't reality television, Uncle Graham," Jason had said, a little defensively. "Are you saying you don't think I am capable of delivering quality?"

"I didn't say that," Uncle Graham had said patiently. "I'm saying that what you do has to be in line with our brand, that's all. And to me, that would mean a program that is capable of winning awards. Art, as it were."

Award-winning art? That was the litmus test? In any given season, dozens of scripts might get tapped by a studio. From those, maybe a third would be made into pilots, and of those, *maybe* as many as two would be ordered to series. Sometimes none. It was damn hard to get picked up, and Jason had done it. Not to mention, creativity didn't flow into neat little packages of award-winning art or trash TV. There were so many things to consider, like the networks and platforms that would take his project and air it. There were so many moving parts, so many things that had to fall in line for this to happen, and the last thing Jason needed was a new bar to hurdle.

"What Uncle Graham is saying is that if it's a bust, we're taking our name and money from the project. That's all." This had come from Jason's younger brother Brock. Brock must have noticed the withering look Jason gave him because he'd smiled and said, "Hey, I totally believe in you, Jase."

"Gee, thanks, Brock."

"We'll need to have the Blackthorne logo on everything you do," Brock had added.

"Like what?" Jason had asked suspiciously.

"I don't know...opening and closing credits? Stationary, payroll, that sort of thing." Jason must have been looking at him like he'd lost his mind because Brock said, "I don't know what all. You tell me."

The whole meeting had pricked at Jason. It wasn't as if he was going to go out and make a reality show, or push something to air that was under-written, overproduced, or poorly acted. It's like he told Mallory that night in his office when they were watching the dailies of the final episode of the first season. "This is exactly what I tried to explain to my family. You start with the vision. You see the characters, you see the narrative arc, right? And you build from there. You can't say at the onset it's going to look exactly like this," he'd said, gesturing at the screen. "This is a work in progress and it slowly builds to what it is. We made that happen."

"I totally get it," Mallory had said. She'd sounded almost dreamy. She'd looked pretty damn dreamy. But then again, they'd had a lot of wine.

Yeah, *that* night. Jason thought about it again, for what had to be the millionth time since it had happened. He'd had a buzz, and he could remember wondering what else Mallory got, and how fucking amazing she looked in that red dress she was wearing, or how her eyes were so blue through her dark-rimmed glasses, and how she always looked half prosecutor, half vixen. She was always adjusting those glasses to take notes. And she was always taking notes. Jason had never known anyone as organized as Mallory Price.

"You do?" he'd asked her that night, like he didn't believe her. "You really get it?"

Mallory had looked at him with surprise, then had held his gaze a long moment. A tiny hint of a smile had tipped up one corner of her mouth. "Yes, Jason, I do. I *really* do."

He didn't know how or why she'd ended up straddling him, but he remembered the way her blue eyes had slid down to his mouth, and how fast he was hard. He remembered the way her breast felt to the palm of his hand. How dense, yet light. He remembered that feeling like a bomb had gone off in him. And he'd been ready to put her on the floor, right there in his office, as someone on the dailies droned on about finding the body on a warehouse floor in a pool of red blood, Jason could feel the red blood in his body, red with desire, spreading through him with the quickness of light.

He had kissed her neck, had felt the flutter of her pulse beneath his lips, and her heat radiate through his hand and up his arm.

Jason had played that night over and over in his mind so many times, alternating between lustful thoughts and remorse, hoping he had not done anything to take advantage of a very late night after a very long day. But sometimes, he looked at Mallory and he just *wanted* her. He always felt so connected to her in a strange way—his disorganization didn't seem to faze her. Her instincts very often matched his. And she was so incredibly desirable. There was a constant air of anticipation when they were in the same room, and that night, it had all come together, and he'd been desperate with want.

Jason hadn't intended it to happen—now he was sounding like Darien in his own head—but he truly hadn't, and that it had happened had surprised him as much as it had surprised her. He could remember having the idea that he ought to drop his hands and move her off his lap, but he'd been invigorated by the scent of vanilla and roses, and his body had hardened, his erection pressing against her thigh. He was too enthralled by what was happening, and he had let his thoughts take flight, imagining them making love in some sultry bedroom lighting, a scene for the ages. He supposed that's why he'd lifted her up and put her on the conference table.

"She was killed with this knife. Looks like she might have been stabbed a dozen or more times in the neck and face."

It had been the dialogue from the dailies, still playing. *Who cares?* Jason had thought, but Mallory had all but gasped in his mouth and had pulled away. She looked at the little screen and then back at Jason. "In the neck and *face*? That seems a bit much. I think we should edit that." And her lips curved into a wonderfully Cheshire little smile of pleasure, and she'd slipped away from him.

And that was that.

They'd never mentioned it again. Specifically, Mallory had not. Jason had waited for her to say something, if not that night, then the day after. And the day after that. But she'd never said a word. She'd acted like it hadn't happened, and therefore, so had he. Like he'd imagined the whole thing.

But Jason thought about it. Real or imagined, he thought about it a lot. He was hyper-aware of Mallory every time she was near. It was as if there was a taut string tethering them to each other.

Yeah, well, given what had happened with Darien and that girl from Calabasas, Jason definitely needed to put Mallory from his mind.

He picked up his jog again, and ran back to the estate to shower. When he was dressed, he answered some emails that had been sent overnight from L.A., then made his way to the kitchen.

He was whipping up a smoothie when his cousin Devlin sauntered in. He stopped when he saw Jason. "What are you doing here?" he asked.

"What do you mean?" Jason said, switching off the

blender. "Please don't tell me you don't remember I was cheering you on in the race."

"Of course I remember, idiot," Devlin said with a playful slap to the back of Jason's head. "But I thought you'd left."

"A better question is, what are you doing here?" Jason asked.

"I just stopped by to pick up a couple of things and check in on Nana." He picked up some mail from the counter and leafed through it.

"Have you heard from Aunt Claire?" Jason asked.

Devlin shook his head.

A little more than two weeks ago, the family had gathered to celebrate Aunt Claire's sixtieth birthday. Jason had had a work crisis in the middle of it—the sound editor was leaving for another gig without notice—so Jason had been a little preoccupied, and had spent most of the night on the terrace on his phone. He didn't know what had happened to spark Aunt Claire, but when he stepped back inside, Aunt Claire had changed clothes and was standing in the door with a suitcase at her feet. Jason didn't hear all what she said, but he could see she and Uncle Graham were at odds, and as he moved into the room, he heard her say, "I'm done putting my life on hold. I've been by your side, in your shadow for way too long. I've kept your secret, even when I knew I shouldn't. It's too much. I can't do it anymore."

Jason wasn't sure what happened next, because his phone had started to ring, and he'd stepped out on the terrace to silence it. When he stepped back in, Aunt Claire was gone and Uncle Graham was telling everyone she was just trying to get through a milestone birthday.

They'd all stood in shock for a long moment, and then everyone was talking at once. Phillip was laughing like it was the funniest thing he'd ever seen.

Well, it was more than facing a milestone birthday, apparently, because that had been a couple weeks ago, and she was still gone. The only thing any of them knew was that she was in Paris. Jason had reached out a few times, but she never responded to his texts or calls.

"So is anyone going to talk to her?" Jason asked Devlin.

"Not right now," he said. "Dad won't go talk to her, and that's who *needs* to go. Right now, she just wants a little space."

"From us," Jason said.

"From everything," Devlin said. He tossed the mail back onto the counter. "How long are you going to be around?"

"A couple of weeks." That's what he hoped. He was going to try and manage the Darien crisis from here. The Netflix brass predictably wanted the issue resolved as soon as possible, especially with Emmy nominations coming up in a couple of months. They'd invested a considerable amount of money in a For Your Consideration campaign plan to garner some *Bad Intentions* nominations. Something like this could definitely derail a carefully planned campaign.

"Good morning."

Devlin and Jason turned toward the door as Uncle Graham strolled into the kitchen. He was nattily dressed, in slim khaki slacks and a crisp white collared shirt.

"Hi, Uncle Graham," Jason said.

"Hey, Dad," Devlin said. "Back to Boston today?"

"Leaving just as soon as I speak to Mother. I need to get out of here, though. The weather is supposed to turn."

"It is?" Jason had really hoped to finish some of the location work today. He was falling behind schedule—a schedule that was all out of whack after just a few days without Mallory to helm it.

"Batten down the hatches, Jase!" Devlin said, and playfully clapped Jason on the shoulder. "It's supposed to be a big one." He said goodbye to them both and left with a hearty, "See you at the Vault!"

When Devlin had left, Graham braced his hands against the bar and leaned forward slightly and settled a fatherly gaze of concern on Jason. His uncle had adopted this habit when Jason's own father and mother had been killed in a plane crash, and he and his brothers had been taken in by their aunt and uncle. Seven boys under one roof. Seven distinct personalities. No wonder Jason felt like he'd bled into the wallpaper.

"So you've got a bit of a problem," Uncle Graham said.

Jason shook his head. "If you're talking about Darien Simmons, I fired him. My assistant should be here this afternoon and we'll start the process of getting someone new on board."

"I'm glad you took action quickly, but that hasn't stopped the tabloids from calling the Blackthorne press office and asking for comment."

"What?" Jason asked reflexively. He'd specifically told Marlene, the Blackthorne Entertainment publicist, to get out in front of it and shield Blackthorne Enterprises. "I'm sorry, I didn't know. We *are* getting ahead of it, Uncle Graham. We'll recast as soon as possible."

Uncle Graham nodded. He walked to the fridge, opened it, and took out a bottle of Perrier. "By the way, I saw the first episode of your show."

There had been so much going on with the Southern Maine Sailing Invitational last week that no one had mentioned Jason's show. He felt a knot form in the pit of his stomach, the same knot he always got before someone passed judgment on his work. "What'd you think?"

"Pretty good," Uncle Graham said. "It certainly held my interest."

Well, it wasn't exactly enthusiastic praise. But it wasn't damning praise, either, and Jason would take it. "It's getting some good buzz."

"Good. I wondered about that. I happened to see a review that called it *Pulp Fiction* for millennials. Whatever that means."

Fantastic. Jason hadn't seen that one yet. There was nothing he enjoyed quite like hearing a new bad review. "We're sitting at 90 percent on Rotten Tomatoes, and that's pretty remarkable for a new series—"

"I have confidence in you, Jason. I just want you to make sure none of this is going to come back on the Blackthorne name."

"I know," Jason said tightly.

"Something like this opens you up for lawsuits, as I am sure you know. It can be very costly very quickly if you aren't proactive."

"I know, Uncle Graham."

He nodded. "Too bad about Darien Simmons. I really liked him in *Comes the Night*."

"Everyone did. He's a great actor. Too bad he's got an issue keeping his fly shut."

"Yes, too bad. You can never guess a man's sexual predilections, can you? But that kind of scandal with less than fantastic ratings?" He shook his head. "Not good."

"We don't have mediocre ratings," Jason said sharply. "We really don't have *any* ratings. This show just started airing. You have to give people time to get invested." He realized that he was arguing about the efficacy of some stupid score on Rotten Tomatoes and then arguing it didn't matter, but Uncle Graham always put him back on his heels.

"I didn't say they were mediocre. I said they weren't fantastic. You know, like one of those *Avenger* movies."

Why did it always feel like Blackthorne Enterprises was pointing a finger at him? Sometimes, this business with the Blackthorne name was too much. It was never about accomplishments, it was always about whatever he was doing had better be damn good. He better not even *think* about besmirching the sacred Blackthorne name.

Uncle Graham was watching him, his brow furrowed. "Did I say something wrong?"

Jason shook his head. "It's a good show. It's not campy, it's not trashy. It's gritty and real and the people at Netflix love it. Darien, we'll deal with. And a bad review here and there is to be expected—you can't please everyone all the time, Uncle Graham. From my perspective, it's going well."

"That's great to hear. But we both know if you lose a star, you lose money. That's just the way things go." He shrugged. He looked at his watch. "I need to get on the road. Check in on your grandmother while you're here, okay?"

"Sure," Jason said. The last time he'd "checked in on" Nana, she'd ended up pouring him into his bed, laughing at how he couldn't hold his whisky.

"All right, Jason, I'll see you soon." Uncle Graham picked up his Perrier and went out the kitchen door, taking the path down to Nana's cottage.

Jason watched him go. Maybe he was defensive, but it always felt like he was held to a higher standard than his cousins or brothers. Phillip, his older brother, just made everything into a prank and laughed about it. And Brock, well, he took it to the other extreme. He was so into the Blackthorne image that he made Jason's art department redo the thistle logo a dozen times before he'd get off their ass.

He shook his head.

When was Mallory getting in? She'd remind him of all the positive news they were getting, of the critical acclaim— at least he hoped there was some critical acclaim. If there was any good news floating around, Mallory would find it. She always had his back that way. She had a lot of positive energy, and she would want to get this Darien thing behind them as quickly as possible.

He paused in the middle of draining his glass. Did he *really* call her at three thirty? He'd make it up to her. He'll get dinner ordered in or something like that. Maybe ask Pam O'Reilly, the housekeeper, if she could arrange something.

He finished his smoothie, picked up his phone, and started making calls.

CHAPTER FOUR

MALLORY BELIEVED THAT FLYING AROUND IN PRIVATE JETS AT the drop of a hat was an incredible waste of both environment and money. She was totally prepared to have her environmental principles completely offended. She was 100 percent going to tell Jason that calling her in the middle of the night to command her to fly to Maine was not only borderline psycho boss behavior, but also meant he didn't truly care about his carbon footprint or the environment.

But then she was distracted by the news coming out about Darien—specifically tweets claiming that the intern wasn't the only woman who had trouble with him. So typical. But what surprised Mallory was that it was *Darien*. If it had been Cass Farenthold, she would have had zero problem believing it.

Cass despised Mallory for reasons she did not really understand, particularly as she'd been perfectly respectful to him. She admired his work. She was thrilled when she got to meet him. But there was that one time when they were casting what was supposed to be a transgender friend of a season one character. The actor Cass wanted was not transgender. Mallory said she thought they ought to ask transgender actors audition. Cass's gaze was cold enough to make her want a parka. He did not take suggestions well.

On the day of shooting, the young actor could not convincingly portray a transgender character, and the writers were sent scrambling to repair the scene. The delay was costly, and since then, Cass could hardly look at her.

Big baby.

Anyway, on the way to the airport, Mallory found her indignation again, and was once again prepared to give Jason a talking to. But this time, she actually stepped onto that private jet, and it was *awesome.*

Mallory could see why people might possibly forget their environmental principles to pass up the crowded airports and shrinking seats and the constant dinging of the wallet by the airlines. She could understand why the lure of wide and soft seats that made into beds made flying fun again. She was *so* glad she'd worn a dress instead of the "sweats" Jason had called her athleisure attire, because it seemed like a flight like this demanded a different sort of vibe. Preferably, a vibe of having some money. She did not have money, but she was a good enough actor to pretend like she did.

The plane had six seats covered in supple leather, a bathroom that was the size of her closet, and recessed overhead lights. The trim was mahogany, the glassware crystal, and even the flight attendant looked like a superior form of human. His name was Chasen, and he was tall and quite fit, and was very solicitous of her, although he wore an expression that suggested he was bored by her. Maybe because he'd seen her type before. Mallory had blurted in her excitement, "This is my first time on a private jet!"

Chasen kindly offered her a pre-flight glass of champagne. But beyond that, he seemed not inclined to share

Mallory's wonder at the marvels of private air travel. He was, however, inclined to show her how her personal lights and television worked, how to put the seat down into a bed, and where the blanket was stowed. And then he dimmed the cabin lights.

Mallory had planned to eat and drink everything that flight offered her. She had intended to luxuriate on the leather seat in full recline position, with five full hours with on-demand movies and television. And she had planned to report back to her friends—nay, *gloat* to her friends. Unfortunately, no thanks to Jason and his middle of the night phone call, and maybe the *two* glasses of champagne she'd very cheerfully allowed Chasen to serve her, she'd fallen asleep almost at once, and didn't wake up until the captain announced they were landing.

The announcement startled her out of a deep sleep, and she was so disoriented for a moment that she jerked up and wrenched her neck. "*Ow,*" she whispered, rubbing her nape. She opened the window shade and looked out as the plane began to descend. They were over ocean—she couldn't see much more than that until the plane touched down. Even then, the only thing she could really see was a rather plain building with one gate and a wind sock on top. Off to the side of the building were two smaller planes, and in the distance, a hangar.

Chasen, from maybe three feet away, pulled down the mic and said, "We've arrived at King Harbor Regional Airport. Please wait until the captain has come to a complete stop before removing your seat belt or standing. Thank you." He hung up the mic.

Of course Mallory waited until the captain had come to a complete stop. She dragged her fingers through her hair and rooted around for her bag. She didn't know what to expect, but that airport looked so small that she was suddenly hoping Jason hadn't stuck her in some fishing cabin for the weekend. She knew the Blackthornes were very wealthy…but she also knew how eccentric wealthy people could be. Hollywood was filled with wealthy weirdos.

When the plane had parked, Chasen opened the door. Someone had rolled steps up to the plane. "I guess this is goodbye," Mallory said to Chasen.

"It is," he confirmed and with his arms folded over his middle, he indicated with his chin she should exit.

"Okay! Thank you!" Mallory stepped out onto the top level of the stairs then proceeded to descend like a celebrity. Unfortunately, no one was around to see her do it.

She continued on, to the tiny terminal.

Inside, there were a few people milling about. There was one airline counter for Caribou Air, and two car rental counters that were manned by the same woman. She waited until a man in a yellow vest delivered her small suitcase, then rolled it the twenty feet across the terminal to the front window. As instructed, she'd placed a call to King Harbor Limos before taking off. The man who'd answered said, "Okay, when did you say you needed pickup?"

Mallory had repeated her flight information.

"Got it. See you then."

"Wait!" Mallory said before he could hang up. "Isn't there a confirmation number or something?"

"A what? No, none of that. I'll be there." And he'd clicked off.

Well, if he was here, he was not presenting himself. She looked around the tiny waiting area, but she didn't see anyone who looked like a driver, no one in a dark suit of clothing. No one holding a brightly lit iPad displaying her name. There was hardly anyone at all.

Mallory took one of eight seats and waited.

And waited.

And waited some more. She tried to call King Harbor Limos, but got no answer. Two passengers leaving King Harbor eventually picked up their bags and walked out on to the tarmac. The rental car agent shut off the lights over her two counters. Mallory pulled out her phone and texted Jason:

At the airport.

She studied the text, wondering if she ought to say more. Like, *Your limo service flaked out on me,* or *I cannot believe you made me fly out here.* While she debated what else to say, three dots appeared on the bottom of her screen. And then vanished.

Mallory frowned. She was starting to worry. The guy behind Caribou Air kept looking at her, then looking at his watch. The terminal, such that it was, was closing up shop and Mallory had been waiting for over an hour.

She used her phone to google a hotel or inn—some place to stay in King Harbor. And then she began to wonder how in hell she would find her way out of King Harbor if Jason had flaked on her and flown off to Boston or—and she'd seriously kill him this time if *that's* what he'd done—when a white van pulled up outside the glass doors and screeched to a stop. The driver door flew open and a mountain of a man bounced out and hurried to the doors of the terminal holding a crumbled piece of paper in his hand. He yanked open the doors like he was late for a flight and then stood with his legs braced apart, looking around. He was wearing a newsboy cap and a leather vest, had a long, scraggly gray beard. He reminded her of someone...*who was it?*

The name suddenly struck her—he looked very much like George RR Martin, the creator of the *Game of Thrones* fantasy series. Mallory's heart skipped a beat. For one tiny moment, she thought Jason might have hired —

"Mallory? Mallory Prince?"

Mallory gained her feet and stood uncertainly. "Price."

He looked at his paper. "Right. Got some cousins in Texas named Prince. Confused you with them." The man adjusted his glasses. "Need a ride to the Blackthorne place, that right?"

That was right. She nodded. Her gaze slid to the plate glass windows and the windowless white van. The man's gaze followed hers. "Flowers."

"Oh. I thought it was supposed to be, ah… I understood it was a limo service?"

"That's my brother. But he's got a…" he made a whirling motion with his hand, "well let's just call it a situation," he said. "So I came to get you. That your bag?" he asked, gesturing to the one at her feet.

"Yes." She picked it up, but he trundled forward and grabbed it from her.

"Come on," he said, moving toward the door. "We're late."

Mallory thought that the "we" in that statement was spreading the blame for being late a little too wide. She hurried to catch up with him, very uncertain about him and this van business. Did no one watch crime shows?

George RR Martin glanced over his shoulder at her. "Are you a Blackthorne?"

"No!" Mallory laughed…but she didn't mean to laugh quite that hard. "I work for a Blackthorne."

"You never know around here," he said. "There's dozens of them if there's one." He held open the door of the terminal for her, then hurried on to the van a few feet away. He slid open the side panel door and Mallory was instantly hit with the strong scent of roses. He shoved her bag behind the

passenger seat and a large cardboard box, then opened the
front passenger seat, picked up a stack of papers and a map
book, and tossed them in the back. "There you go." He didn't
wait for her to get in—he was already hurrying around to the
driver's side of the van as if he suspected the airport was
going to blow at any moment.

Mallory hesitated. This van, those flowers—Jason had
said a *limo* service. It didn't seem particularly smart to get in
a flower delivery van with a man who was not the limo
driver. Which, come to think of it, was not a bad premise for
an episode of *Bad Intentions*. She'd just make a quick note on
her phone.

George RR Martin climbed into the driver's seat, picked
up a clipboard and jotted something down, then tossed it onto
the dash. He cranked up the van then looked at Mallory, still
standing where he'd left her. "Well? Come on, now, we're
already late. We got some weather moving in."

She glanced at the sky. It was sunny and blue with some
stripes of clouds across it. She glanced back. The airport was
definitely closing and she hadn't figured out a lot of options.
So she got in.

"The name is Ned," he said.

"Hi Ned."

"You been out to the Blackthorne place before?"

"Never."

"Nice drive. Scenic, if you're into oceans."

She was into oceans. Who wasn't into oceans?

Ned wasn't kidding about the scenic part. He took a route
along the rocky coastline. The tide was coming in, great
waves crashing against the cliffs. They passed two lighthouses, and in the distance she could see trawlers and sailboats bobbing on the surface.

They entered a quaint fishing village with a wooden sign

that proclaimed it to be King Harbor. It looked like something you'd see on a postcard, a colorful fishing village that looked rustic and quaint with it's Cape Cod-style houses facing the water, the fish and tackle shops along the docks. The harbor was calm, the surface smooth, and boats were peacefully anchored, hardly moving at all.

Ned drove past restaurants that boasted the best Maine clam chowder. Several of them advertised the availability of Blackthorne whisky. From one shop, a colorful array of wind socks in the shape of fish dangled along the overhang. Shop windows were filled with miniature lighthouses at varying sizes, and of course, red lobsters were the symbol of most businesses.

After they had gone through the village, Ned turned left onto a narrower road. It wended around the cliffs and through thick stands of trees until they came to a halt outside a tall white wooden gate. "Here you are," Ned said, and put the van in park.

"Here we are?" Mallory said, but Ned was already out the driver door.

She got out of the van as Ned retrieved her suitcase. With his chin and beard, he indicated the gate. "You'll find the Blackthorne place through there."

Mallory looked at the gate and the *No Trespassing* sign. "Through there. There's a sign that says no trespassing."

"Just a warning."

She blinked. "But isn't there a door or something?"

Ned looked a little exasperated. "Look, it's on the other side of that gate, and there ain't much space between us and the ocean. You'll find it well enough. Just go through the smaller gate there," he said, and pointed to a small door next to the big gates. He rolled her suitcase to her, then hurried back to the driver's seat.

Mallory stood dumbly and watched him back the van up and drive off with a cheery wave, leaving her utterly alone on that road on the wrong side of a big wooden gate.

She took out her phone and phoned Jason. No answer. He'd probably misplaced his phone. "Predictable," she muttered.

She adjusted her backpack, gripped her suitcase, and walked to the small door in the fence and tried the handle. It was open. She stepped through to a jungle of overgrowth on the other side. "This is not the Blackthorne place!" she shouted in exasperation. The undergrowth grew up and over the footpath. But she could see a road, and she managed to get her bag down the uneven path to a drive. Given how many weeds were poking up through the asphalt, this didn't bode well. She pictured some sort of *Grey Gardens* scenario. Rolling her suitcase behind her, Mallory started down the asphalt road, glancing back over her shoulder every now and then, sort of wishing Ned would come through and pick her up. The wind had picked up quite a bit, and it felt as if her hair was standing straight up because of it. Plus, it was a fairly steep road, and her suitcase kept bumping into her heel.

The road slowly began to curve, and as it did, the top of a massive structure came into view.

She could see a roof. And then…a hotel? But it had dormers and a widow's walk. An inn? It had to be—this looked much bigger than a house. Had Jason ever mentioned a Blackthorne inn or resort?

Her phone suddenly startled her and she almost killed herself trying to get it out of her pocket. "*Jason!*" she shouted into the phone.

"Whoa, that was *loud*," Jason said. "Where are you?"

"Walking down a road toward this inn. Where are you?"

"Mallory? Are you there? I can't hear you—you're breaking up."

"I'm on a road!" she shouted.

"Text me when you get here."

"That's what I'm saying. I think I'm—"

"Wow, the reception is really bad, Mallory. You're all garbled. TEXT ME WHEN YOU GET HERE," he shouted, and clicked off.

"Wait!" She hurried down the road trying to get a better signal, but it was too late—he'd hung up. "Damn it, Jason," she muttered. That was so like him, rushing from one thing to another, couldn't give it ten seconds to see if she could get to a better signal.

She walked on, annoyed now, watching the inn or whatever it was get larger and larger until she was standing right outside another, smaller gate in a white picket fence. The fence surrounded a garden. Attached to the garden was a Cape Cod cottage with dormer windows and a porch that faced the sea. It was so picturesque.

She noticed a small woman with a head full of white hair, dressed in red sneakers and clam diggers, wandering through the garden. Mallory hadn't seen an actual pair of clam diggers since she was a girl.

The garden the woman was wandering was bursting with color. She seemed to be focused on the peonies and rhododendrons, clipping off dead leaves, filling a bucket with the blooms. There were hollyhocks that stood as tall as her, and patches of larkspur and foxglove so thick that Mallory worried she'd get lost in them. Mallory would bet that old lady knew everything there was to know about the rhododendrons she was bent over.

She parked her suitcase, adjusted her backpack onto her

shoulder, and began to walk toward the woman on the gravel path. "Hello!" she called.

The woman turned around and stared at Mallory. Her clear blue eyes were filled with curiosity, as if she thought she might know Mallory from somewhere. Or maybe didn't know her at all.

Mallory smiled to put her at ease. "Do you work here?" she asked as she drew closer. She looked around the garden. "It's so pretty."

"Do I *work* here?" the woman asked incredulously. "I most certainly do not."

Mallory blanched. "I'm sorry. I just thought that you… you were working on the rhododendrons and I…" *Okay, back it up.* "I was looking for Jason Blackthorne. I think he's staying here?"

"Well of course he is. It's his home."

Mallory tried gamely to compute that statement. Jason's family lived in an inn? Were they maybe innkeepers? She looked over her shoulder and studied the structure. That wasn't an inn for the rich and famous, it was a *house* for the rich and famous. It wasn't as if Mallory hadn't seen giant houses—she lived in L.A. after all. But this was so huge and so charming, with so many nooks and crannies and angles and windows and doors. And the widow walk! It looked like an expensive inn. The kind that had been converted to a treatment facility where celebrities were sent to recover from "exhaustion."

Mallory had heard Jason was whisky rich, which, okay, Mallory didn't really know what that meant. He had a respectable house in Hollywood Hills—she'd had to deliver scripts to him once. But this house was a whole other level, and never in a million years would she guess whisky was this kind of rich.

"You better go let him know you're here," the woman said, waving toward the house. "You don't want to get caught in a storm."

Mallory looked up at the spring sky. Wavy puffs of white clouds were bunching together over the ocean.

"That's a mackerel sky," the woman pointed out, apparently sensing Mallory's skepticism. She leaned down and picked up a bucketful of rhododendrons and peonies. "Go knock on the door. He'll come if he's home. I'm Fiona, by the way."

"Hi," Mallory said, and extended her hand. "I'm Mallory."

Fiona gripped her hand with surprising strength. "Go on, now." With her bucket, she went out the gate and up the steps of the cottage, disappearing inside.

Mallory went back to fetch her suitcase and dragged it over the gravel. But the gravel kept locking the wheels, and the case knocked into her knee. So she hoisted it in her hand and walked out of the garden and to the stairs leading up to the porch.

If the house had a grand entrance, she wasn't seeing it. There was a single door behind a screen. Mallory dragged her suitcase up the steps and rolled it in front of her to the door. She dragged her fingers through her hair in an attempt to tame it as she studied the door before her. Frankly, it looked like a servant's entrance. She was tempted to dig out her phone and text Inez a picture of this house and that door. But Inez was on set today, and Mallory didn't want to explain that she'd jetted out to Maine on Jason's demand. She could already hear the *I told you sos*.

Mallory looked around for a doorbell, and finding nothing obvious, she knocked.

She waited.

She leaned to her right to peer in through a sidelight window, but could see nothing but hardwood floors covered in thick rugs, a console table against one of the hall walls with a vase full of peonies. She knocked again, only louder this time.

Still, no one came. "*Damn* it, Jason," she muttered beneath her breath. "Why is everything about you so hard?" She fully intended to add this trip through the Maine countryside to the long list of things she had to say to Jason about this whole ordeal. Which included, *do you know everyone talks about how insane you are?* And *If you summon me to Maine, could you at least be somewhere IN Maine?*

She turned to go. To where, she had no idea, and she was beyond furious as she pondered how difficult it would be to get a cab here—her guess was very—when the door suddenly swung open and Jason was standing before her in gym shorts.

And nothing else.

He was shirtless. *He was not wearing a shirt.* Whatever Mallory had been thinking was gone from her head and, for the record, Jason Blackthorne without a shirt was…inspiring. She tried to avert her gaze from his impressive form, but she couldn't seem to make herself do it. It was like she had cartoon googly eyes glued to his chest. Heretofore, Mallory had not seen Jason shirtless. She had guessed at his abs, of course, because he wore his clothes very tight and it was impossible not to notice. She had certainly noticed the night she'd crawled on his lap how firm and broad his chest and shoulders looked in his blue shirt that seemed to lack the capacity to contain his arms. But to see him so blatantly bare, so chiseled and hard and completely within reach was enough to make her take a step back. To see the shadow of hair on his chest, and the other, tantalizing line of furry down that disappeared into the elastic of his shorts, was enough to leave her speechless. Mallory stared at him.

Jason apparently didn't see the issue. He scrubbed at the nape of his neck and frowned at her. "Why are you looking at me like you've never met me? And why didn't you call or text? I would have come out and helped you."

In a supreme effort to stop ogling her boss's chest, Mallory made herself look at his eyebrows. "I tried. You said I was breaking up."

He swept two fingers across his brow, as if he thought something was there.

"I thought this was an inn. But the little old lady in the garden—"

"Nana."

"What?"

"That was my grandmother. Nana. She was picking flowers, right? Didn't she tell you who she was?"

"She said her name was Fiona. And something about a mackerel sky? And that you lived in this house, which I thought was an inn."

Jason looked past her, dipping a little to see the sky. "Yep. That's a mackerel sky all right. You thought this was an inn?" He laughed. "This is not an inn. Why are you coming through the garden, anyway? You should have come in the front door. I thought you were calling the limo service."

"Right. About that limo—it was a *windowless van*. Do you have any idea what kind of shenanigans go on in windowless vans? You said limo!"

"I said limo *service*," he corrected her. "Sometimes they have cars and sometimes, Ned drives. But usually, they come to the front of the house," he said, hooking a thumb over his shoulder in the opposite direction.

"Well Ned the van guy let me out at a big gate on top of the hill."

"Huh," Jason said thoughtfully. Then he shrugged. "He must have been in a hurry. That's the back way in. Why didn't you call me?"

Mallory gave him a withering look. "I did," she said. "Like ten minutes ago. I am so *mad* at you right now."

"You'll get over it," he said with cheerful confidence. Because Jason said everything with cheerful confidence. He pushed the screen door to stand open on its own and then arranged himself with one arm braced high against the doorjamb and studied her up and down. "You look tired, Mal."

"Ya think? Someone woke me at three thirty and made me get a on a plane."

Jason smiled, all dimples and showy white teeth. "It's a pretty sweet ride, isn't it?"

She wanted to argue, but she couldn't. "*So* sweet," she admitted. "Every man, woman and child ought to be able to fly like that."

"What about the carbon footprints?"

"Shut up." She'd take on responsible stewardship of the environment another day.

His grin deepened. "So come in. You look like you could use a drink." He turned away from the door, walking into the house. "I just finished in the gym. Are you hungry? I'm starving. I had Pam order something in for dinner. Should arrive fairly soon."

Mallory tried to maneuver her suitcase inside, but the screen door shut in her face.

"Oh, sorry," Jason said instantly and dipped back, pushed open the screen, and grabbed her bag.

"I really think I should check in, don't you?"

"Check in? Check in where?"

"Check in…at a hotel." Was it possible that Jason had actually thought ahead to that? No. Not possible.

"What are you talking about? You'll stay here." He picked up her suitcase as if it weighed nothing and walked down a wide corridor. "Look at this place. It's enormous."

"I can't stay with your family," she said, laughing at the absurdity of it.

"Family? There's no one here but me."

"Why? Have they gone somewhere?"

He looked back at her as if she wasn't speaking English. "It's a summerhouse. I'm the only one here this week."

Well that made no sense to Mallory's very lower middle-class self. She could not fathom a summerhouse this big and this empty, and she had to pause to look around her to absorb the idea. If she had a summerhouse with large picture windows that framed a view of the ocean from every room that she could see, she'd be right here. She looked at the boxed beam ceilings, and hand-scraped hardwood floors. At the two-sided fireplace made of river rock. The furnishings were just as grand—chairs and sofas made of leather and brocade, and thick wool rugs to cover sections of the floor. And the kitchen! It looked like a set from an old Nora Ephron movie, with high-end appliances and marble countertops. "I can't stay here, Jason."

He seemed confused. "Why not?"

She didn't know how to explain that a girl from a very small house and a very big family should not be in a fancy house like this. *This* was beyond her reach, and she instinctively recoiled from reaching. Maybe because she'd grown up at or near the poverty level.

But it was more than that, if she was being honest. Jason wasn't wearing a shirt, and the busy little bees that maintained her libido were working overtime and had kicked it up a notch.

He frowned. "You've got that look on your face."

"What look?"

"You know, that look you get."

"Are you referring to the look I get that is my face?" she asked irritably as she tried to figure out what look he was talking about.

"Look, Mallory, is this about…" He hesitated, pressed his lips together a moment, as if he was trying to think of what to say. "You don't have to…" He hesitated again, and Mallory wondered if he was talking about that night in his office. *Oh God.* She could feel the color creeping up her neck and into her face. *Please don't say it.* "Look, if you want to stay in town, we'll drive in later and get you a room."

Interestingly, uber-confident Jason looked strangely embarrassed, which was a look on him she'd never seen. Oh God—had she embarrassed him that night? That's what she got for trying to play vixen. She generally tried not to think about that night at all, because she'd been so mortified by it, but it was damn difficult to forget when he was standing here and now without his shirt. "Thanks," she muttered, and looked at her feet. "It's not that I don't appreciate…I mean, I think it's probably not…" *Shut up. Shut up shut up shut up.* She was getting weirder and weirder and she didn't like it. She suddenly looked up. "You know what? I could really use a bathroom. Do you have a bathroom I could use?"

He stared at her for a long moment, almost as if he was debating something, and she could feel his gaze penetrating hers, could feel it sliding merrily down into her groin. But then he nodded toward a door in the hall. "It's right in there," he said. Then he pointed at a door the other way. "I'll be in there. Kitchen is on the other side of the dining room." He deposited her suitcase in the hall and disappeared into the dining room.

Mallory slipped into the powder room, leaned over the sink, and splashed water on her face. When she glanced up, she recoiled. Her short hair was going in all directions. She had dark circles under her eyes from a lack of sleep. And her pulse was pounding in her neck because Inez was right—she was a cake around very handsome, sexy men. "For the love of Pete," she muttered. She was definitely going to need him to put on a shirt and get a room in town if she was going to survive this unexpected trip to Maine. She was only human.

And she was still pissed, too, she realized. Maybe as pissed as she was this morning. Was it only this morning? She paused to think about that. It seemed so long ago now. But on top of waking her up, making her fly to Maine, he'd answered the door looking ridiculously and mouthwateringly hot and inviting her to stay in this ridiculously fancy *summer*house.

Yep. She was mad all over again.

CHAPTER FIVE

HE CLEARLY MADE HER UNCOMFORTABLE. JASON HADN'T realized before today how uncomfortable he made her. In all the weirdness that followed that night in the office, he thought she'd just sort of blithely put it behind her, but obviously, she had not.

He walked down the hall to the gym and rooted around in a closet until he found a shirt in a basket. He put it to his nose. Not too bad. He slipped it on over his head and looked down. It was an old Harvard T-shirt he figured had belonged to his brother Phillip. In this house, anything left behind was fair game.

He returned to the kitchen and took down a bottle of whisky, pouring a finger of it for himself. Mallory looked really tired, and he felt pretty guilty about that. His thoughts could be so scattered sometimes, especially when he was busy. After his parents had died, and Jason hadn't been able to absorb his grief, Aunt Claire had suggested maybe he had ADHD. He didn't have ADHD—he'd had a full-blown case of missing his parents and a desire to drown his feelings about their sudden loss.

But he was very disorganized. He'd had girlfriends through the years who, when he forgot to call, would accuse him of being unfeeling and inconsiderate. He forgot to call not because he was intentionally unfeeling, but because he walked around with a jumble of ideas in his head, and the more interesting thoughts crowded out the more mundane. Some people could deal with all those thoughts at once, but he was not one of them.

Mallory understood that about him. She walked around behind him, picking up the forgotten cell phone, or finding his lost keys. Her super organizational skills were a perfect match for his inability to organize even a sock drawer. And there was that curious mix of prosecutor and sex kitten all wrapped up one. From the moment she'd walked into his office, he had felt a twinge deep and low. He remembered that day. She was wearing a dress, and she looked fantastic, and she had legs that stretched into next week. But she was all prim and proper, holding onto that binder for dear life. She had said all the right things…but she'd said them to his mouth, and he had wondered if she hadn't felt that twinge, too.

He knew there were times he took advantage of her efficiency, but he really didn't mean to. Like today, making her fly out here at the last minute. And she'd arrived bedraggled and miffed, and then she'd been intimidated by the size of this house. If there was one thing he got about Mallory, it was that she liked to know what to expect. And she had not expected this house.

Jason tended to forget how the Blackthorne life looked to outsiders. This house, in particular, was large, and he could understand why someone might think it was a tony inn in Maine on the waterfront. It reeked of old money and a past grandeur that few experienced.

But to a Blackthorne, this house was also a family treasure, built to house generations. It was home, it was summer, and in a family that had come to include seven boys, there had been many times it hadn't seemed quite big enough.

He looked around the kitchen. Aunt Claire had had the kitchen renovated several years ago, and it looked like something out of *Architectural Digest* with its marble countertops, white cabinetry, and gleaming stainless appliances. There was an office and even a library in the house, neither of which had a view of the ocean, so Jason had set up a makeshift office at the kitchen table. From there, he had a spectacular view of the Atlantic and the sailboats that bobbed by every day.

In the mornings, he often worked on the flagstone patio and made his calls as the sun slowly climbed to a noon sky. There was one thing he could say for King Harbor, and that was that it was peaceful here. Quiet. Nothing but the sound of the sea churning into land below the house to distract him. After several years in Los Angeles, it was a welcome respite from the hustle and bustle.

He'd thoroughly enjoyed his time here until Darien pulled his shit.

And then he discovered Mallory was apparently afraid to be alone with him. That unsettling comparison to Darien made him nauseous.

He heard the door of the hall bathroom close. A moment later, Mallory found her way to the kitchen. She'd combed her hair and washed her face. She smiled sheepishly, drew a breath and said, "Starting over. This house is amazing, Jason."

"Thanks. We like it."

"Did you grow up here?"

She was trying to diffuse her anxiety and exasperation with small talk. He would play along. "I grew up in Boston, actually, but we spent our summers here. You can put your backpack down, you know."

"Huh?" She turned slightly, as if trying to see her back. As if she'd forgotten she was carrying the backpack. She slid it off her shoulder, wincing when she did, then looked around, uncertain where to put it while she tried to massage her own shoulder.

"For heaven's sake," Jason said. He walked around from behind the kitchen bar, took it from her, and plopped it into a chair.

"Thanks," Mallory said.

"I can help with that," Jason said.

"With what?

"Your shoulder. Your muscles are tense from carrying it around all day. I could massage it out for you."

"Oh, that's okay," she said.

He shrugged. "Fine. But it would feel a lot better."

"Okay," she said. "It's really tight."

"I can tell." Jason made a circle motion with his finger. "Turn around."

She presented her back to him and Jason put his hands on her shoulders and began to knead the tension from her muscles.

"Oh," Mallory said. "*Oh!*" She dropped her head. "Oh my *God*," she breathed.

Jason clenched his teeth. He wished she wouldn't make moaning sounds quite like that. They sparked through him, making him think of things he did not want to be thinking about with his assistant. Jesus, he'd just fired Darien! He'd just been mentally chastising himself for the night in his office. But her neck, slender and smooth, was exposed to him, and he could not stop looking at it. Could not stop thinking about pressing his lips against it.

He was such a pig.

"Wow, Jason," she said.

"Why are you so *tight*?" he asked. He was also tight. Wound to a tight coil imagining his lips lingering at the top of her spine, then moving down that spine, one vertebra at a time.

Mallory groaned loudly when he dug this thumbs into the spot where her shoulders curved into her neck. She began to whimper—he could feel the tension releasing from her muscle. "You're surprisingly good at this."

"Surprisingly?" He chuckled.

"I wouldn't have guessed you as a massage kind of guy. I would have guessed you the kind of guy who is always on the receiving end of a massage."

She wasn't wrong. "Fair," he said. He wondered if there was anything about him Mallory hadn't figured out. "But I know how to give a massage—I'm not a heathen." Except when he was. He sighed. "So listen, I'm really sorry about last night. I wasn't thinking."

"Technically, it was this morning, but thank you." She tilted her head to one side. "In all honesty, I had a speech I was prepared to make, but my shoulders haven't felt his relaxed in weeks. So you're off the hook."

He smiled at the back of her head. He stopped kneading her muscles and let his hands drop. Mallory didn't move. She stood in the very same spot with her back to him, swaying a little.

"Are you all right?"

"Yes." She turned around with a smile of gratitude, but he was standing so close that she almost bumped into him when she did. They were standing so close that he could actually feel the pull between them. It felt strangely magnetic, and it was the same he always felt around her.

It didn't help that Mallory's lips were slightly parted, and her blue eyes were shining through her glasses. Jason was totally there for the sexy vibe, but it felt as if an elephant was trying to squeeze in between them. "Mallory, I feel like I—"

"Hell-*oooh*!"

Mallory jumped back so fast that her centrifugal force nearly knocked Jason off his feet. In the next moment, Pam O'Reilly, the estate's housekeeper, appeared carrying a dish in a quilted insulation bag. "Oh! I wasn't sure you were in," she said. "I have a delivery for you. Lobster risotto!"

Jason looked at the covered dish. It didn't look like any delivery service he knew. "Where'd that come from?"

"From my kitchen," Pam said proudly. She turned her smile to Mallory.

"Oh, sorry," Jason said with a shake of his head. "Pam, this is Mallory Price, my assistant." To Mallory he said, "Pam O'Reilly. She and her husband Joe are the caretakers here."

"Pleased to meet you," Mallory said like a woman who had been sent to finishing school, and then she marched forward to extend her hand like a woman who'd been raised in a sales force.

Pam smiled with delight. "Well, it's a pleasure to meet you, too, Mallory." She put down the dish and shook Mallory's hand enthusiastically.

"Thanks for this, Pam," Jason said. "But you shouldn't have gone to any trouble. I meant order out."

"This is nothing," she said with a flick of her wrist. "And it's a lot easier than getting something from a restaurant. They make you wait so long these days. Now, this is warm, but you can heat it up a little if necessary. It should be all right in this insulated cover for a bit. Very nice to meet you, Mallory," she said again. She turned her attention to Jason. "I'm going to check in on Fiona. Would you like me to come back and clean the kitchen?"

"God, no," Jason said quickly. They may have grown up with a host of staff to do whatever the family needed, but as an adult, he didn't care for it. He was a single man and he didn't need anyone to clean his kitchen. "You can correct whatever I did wrong tomorrow." He winked at Pam and said to Mallory, "Pam likes the kitchen to be a certain way."

Pam laughed. "That's not true at all. But there are too many men who come through here and throw things into drawers without even trying to put them back where they should obviously go. Oh, look at the time! I better go. It's going to storm soon. Have a good evening!" she said cheerfully, and hurried out the way she'd come.

"She's an excellent cook," Jason said.

"I have no doubt," Mallory said. "I can smell it from here and I am about to pass out from hunger. Should we make a salad? I'm very good at that sort of thing," she said, glancing at her watch.

"I can make a salad."

"I can whip one out in no time—"

"We're not in a race, Mal," Jason said. "I can make a salad. Will you relax?"

She eyed him suspiciously. "You don't seem like a kitchen guy to me. I figured you'd have people to do that."

She didn't think he was the type to give massages, she didn't think he could make a salad. What did she think of him, then? "I know my way around the kitchen," he said, a little defensively. She was right—there always had been "people to do that," but when his parents had died, and they'd moved in with their cousins, he'd had to learn. There were just so many boys and so many needs. At times, it had felt like he was living in a boarding house—every man for himself. How many times had he come in from baseball practice only to find the meal over and nothing left for him, because no one had noticed him missing? Or had noticed too late. He'd had to learn to fend for himself.

He didn't like to think about that time in his life. It brought back painful memories of loss.

"Well...okay, if you insist. But I'm happy to help," Mallory said, and glanced at her watch again.

Mallory liked her schedule. It was usually one of the things Jason appreciated about her most, and God knew he dreaded telling her what he'd done to the production schedule. But tonight she was annoying him with it. He glanced out the windows as he walked around the kitchen bar. The wind had picked up and the sea was beginning to cap. "We have time," Jason said. "And we've got a lot of work to do, too. But right now, I am hungry. Want a drink? If you like whisky, Blackthorne is the best."

"No thank you," Mallory said primly. "I have a rule about working and drinking. The two don't mix."

"Interesting new rule," he drawled, because they both knew she hadn't had a problem drinking that night in his office.

Mallory's cheeks colored slightly. "I didn't say I'm very good about following my rules, but, you know, it's getting late."

"Is it?" He picked up the drink he'd poured for himself and sipped.

Mallory looked at his drink, then at the window. "I think I should find some place soon if it's really going to storm. I'm just going to have a look if that's okay." She leaned over her backpack and pulled out an iPad as Jason started to gather the ingredients for a salad. She slipped onto a seat at the bar and typed something into her iPad. "Here is the King Harbor Arms," she said.

"Flop house," Jason said.

"Oh." She leaned a little closer to her device. "A Holiday Inn—"

"On the highway," Jason said. "Closed for renovations. They'll reopen in a couple of weeks."

"Huh." She kept scrolling. "What about the Pirate's Cove Inn?"

"Sure, if you don't mind the smell of fish. It's next to the pier." He glanced up and smiled a little lopsidedly. "And that's where Cass is staying."

"Ugh," Mallory said with a cute wrinkle of her nose. "So does this mean all of the hotels in King Harbor are undesirable?"

He stuck a head of lettuce under the faucet. "It means the best place for you to stay is right here."

"Still not a good idea," she said, and with her brow furrowed, she turned back to her list.

"By the way," Jason said. "I had to rearrange a few things on the production schedule."

Mallory's head came up slowly. "You *what*?"

"Don't freak out."

"Don't freak—what have you done, Jason?" She phrased the question as if she had just discovered him standing over a dead body, holding a gun. "You know how you are with schedules. You don't know how they work—"

"I know how schedules work." He began to tear the lettuce and toss it in a bowl.

"Not production schedules. Remember when you changed the shooting sequence for episode ten of season one and the gaffer almost quit?"

"A, that was a misunderstanding, and B, in hindsight, we should have fired him anyway."

"Yeah, well, some say misunderstanding, some say—"

"Okay, all right," he interjected before she could repeat what half the crew thought of him for that gaffe. "We went over it at the time. No need to repeat all the opinions." He believed her exact word had been *moron*.

"My point is, you shouldn't be messing with schedules."

He looked at her with incredulity and tried not to be distracted by how cute she looked right now. "You do realize that I have single-handedly created a production company, right? Anyway, I am sure you can work with what I've done because you *are* a genius with schedules."

She grinned. "I *am* good," she agreed. "And perceptive, too. I always know when I am being buttered up like an ear of corn." She arched a brow at him.

Jason laughed and began to toss the salad.

Mallory consulted her watch.

"Will you relax? We'll be done here in half an hour." He put the salad aside, took the casserole dish from the insulated bag, and removed the lid. Mallory's gaze fell to the contents. She looked like she might crawl across the bar for it.

"Looks good, right?" he asked mildly, and turned to a cabinet for plates.

"It looks like something I would be perfectly happy to face-plant in," Mallory said. "Not that I would. But I could."

Jason found a serving spoon and dished some of the risotto onto a plate. He added salad, then handed the plate to her. "We could eat on the terrace."

"Great idea." She took the plate and walked outside.

He joined her a moment later with his plate, a couple of forks and napkins, and his whisky.

"So tell me about Darien," she said as they settled in. "What do we need to do?"

"Eat," he said firmly, pointing at her plate.

"It is possible to accomplish two things at once."

"It's also possible to take a break. I've been on the phone all day about Darien and even if you won't take a moment to breathe, I'd like one. Plus, I feel like I haven't eaten in a month."

"Same," she said, and forked risotto into her mouth. She immediately closed her eyes and moaned. "Oh my God. This is so good. Isn't this good?" She forked another, healthier bite.

"Pam makes the best risotto," Jason agreed.

"Where does she live?"

"Here, in a cottage on the property. Next door to Nana, actually."

"Why doesn't your grandmother live in this house?" Mallory asked curiously.

"I don't know," Jason said. "I think she likes having a place to herself. And she doesn't like stairs. This place has a lot of stairs. In her cottage, she's closer to Pam and her husband Joe when no one else is around."

The sound of thunder in the distance brought their attention to the ocean. The clouds were building over the ocean, but they hadn't turned menacing yet, which meant the storm was developing behind them. Mallory turned back to her food. "So everyone comes here for the summer?" she asked before another big bite.

"Yep. Some weeks the house is full. Like last week—my cousin, Devlin, raced in the Southern Maine Sailing Invitational."

"How fun! I've never been on a sailboat. Did he win?"

Jason chuckled. Devlin didn't win the race, but he'd definitely won the girl. "In a manner of speaking. He and my uncle Graham came in second. He's really good. So fill me in —what's going on in the office this week?"

"Oh, the office." She shook her head. "Ye old Peyton Place as always. So you know Jericho has been—" She was startled by a louder clap of thunder and jerked her gaze to the ocean again. "But the sky is—"

A gust of wind hit them so hard that a cloth napkin and little pot of marigolds went flying off the table. On the backside of the house, it was often hard to tell anything was happening with the weather until it was right on top of you.

"Oh no!" Mallory cried. "I have to get to town, Jason!"

As if on cue, the skies opened and the rain began to pour down from what seemed like giant buckets. Jason grabbed their plates. Mallory was right behind him with his drink and the silver.

Another, bone-rattling clap of thunder made her shriek. She put the things she had on the kitchen table, then hurried to her backpack.

"What are you doing?" Jason asked, confused.

"I have some weather apps!"

"Apps? As in plural?" A streak of lightning flashed in through the windows. A heartbeat later it was followed by another clap of thunder that rattled the windowpanes. Rain began to fall sideways, lashing at the house.

Mallory looked wide-eyed at Jason. She turned the screen of her phone to him and showed him what he assumed was a weather app. The entire screen was red.

"That settles it," he said. "You're staying here tonight." He picked up a bottle of whisky from the kitchen counter with a glossy black label and gold lettering that read *Blackthorne Reserve*. "Now will you have that drink?"

CHAPTER SIX

SHE SHOULD HAVE KNOWN HE'D GET HIS WAY, EVEN IF HE HAD to usher in a storm to do it. Mallory stared at the bottle of whisky he was holding. And at her half-eaten meal, which he'd set down beside a laptop and a mess of papers and ledgers and printed pages from digital storyboards on the kitchen table. Outside, the day had gone almost black, it was raining so hard.

Yep, it definitely looked like she was stuck here for the night. Which, all things considered, was a fabulous place to be stuck. Just not if you had a crush on the only man in the house. She sighed. "I told you I needed to get a room sooner rather than later. Now look what's happened."

"It's not *that* bad," he said, clearly offended.

"No! Your house is beautiful. It's just…I don't want to impose."

"Jesus, Mallory, you're not imposing. How can you be imposing on an empty house?"

He had a point. How did she explain she couldn't stay here because she was ridiculously attracted to him and all she could think about were his abs right now?

Jason lowered the bottle. He braced both hands against the kitchen bar and pinned her with a look. "Listen, Mallory, I think we need to address the elephant here."

"*What?* No, Jason. Don't address any elephants! All the elephants are perfectly happy roaming around and do not need to be addressed."

He arched a brow. "Clearly they do."

Mallory groaned.

"This…elephant anxiety you're having has to do with that night in the office, doesn't it?"

She said nothing.

"Because if that's what is bothering you, I swear to God, I will be a perfect gentleman. I cannot apologize enough for having…for having made you uncomfortable." Wait. That sounded like he thought she was worried about him being a gentleman. She was worried about *her* being a gentleman. What was she going to say? She should come clean. Except that was a *horrible* idea. Talk about elephants—that would invite an entire heard into the room.

Her inability to speak seemed only to agitate Jason more. "I'll put you in a room with your own bath. You can lock the door. Pull a dresser in front of it if that makes you feel better."

Wow. She didn't know he felt that way, and by "that way," she meant guilty. What did he have to be guilty about? She was the one who'd climbed on his lap.

"I could ask Nana to come up and—"

"No!" This was escalating quickly. "I would never ask you to fetch your grandmother in this storm," she said, biding for time so she could think. "And besides, you have it all wrong, Jason. I'm not afraid of you. That's, like, the exact opposite of what I am."

His brow furrowed, as if he didn't know what she meant.

Okay, there was clearly no way to get out of this, exactly. So she would have to be very vague. "Think about it. I climbed on your lap, remember?"

Jason's gaze flicked over her body. He swallowed. "Actually, I remember very clearly," he said in a low voice.

A strange little sizzle shot through her. She remembered, too. "We both had too much to drink, and while you were a full participant, it was me. All me."

"I don't think—"

Mallory threw up a hand. "Can we just let it drop? I feel bad enough about it, obviously, and I've tried to be very respectful since."

"No, we can't let it drop. Because I need to know if you really thought it was *all you*, why are you so reluctant to stay here tonight? I thought it was because you didn't trust me."

She didn't want to confess that it was herself she didn't trust. She didn't want to come off as a sex-crazed lunatic. She was not a lunatic.

"And if you don't trust me, then this arrangement is not going to work. We've danced around it long enough, Mallory. You've been different with me since that night. You act like it never happened but we both know it did."

"Okay," she said, holding up a hand. "Okay, that is true. I know I did that, and I…I wish I could explain it, but it's hard to explain."

He waited for her to say more, but she couldn't think of what to say. "Try," he insisted. "Because all this time, I've believed you were too afraid to confront me and tell me I acted inappropriately, because maybe you thought that I would somehow threaten your job if you did—"

"I never thought that!"

"It's the only explanation that has made any sense." He

was talking more to himself than her. "I mean, unless you had a real thing for me." He chuckled as if that was a ridiculous assumption. "You joked about having a crush on me, but that was the wine talking."

Mallory stood frozen with alarm.

Jason's grin began to fade. He studied her a moment. "Jesus. Mallory?" He shifted toward her, his hazel-eyed gaze locked firmly on hers. She could feel it surging through her. "*Mallory,*" he said in a whisper. "Are you...*Do* you have a real thing for me?"

"No." She laughed. Jason didn't laugh. He kept looking right through her. And she could feel the heat rising in her like a hot summer day. She laughed again, but too hard, and there was no mistaking that laugh. That was a-guilty-as-charged laugh.

Jason's expression changed, morphing from realization, to curiosity, and then to confusion. "But—"

"Yeah, okay," she said, waving her hand at him. "Don't get it twisted. I don't have a *thing* for you, Jason," she lied. "But I'm a healthy woman, and you're a very good-looking man, and I didn't expect you to look like that when you opened the door. That's all."

"Like what?"

She jumped at another loud clap of thunder. "Shirtless. And..." She gave him a bit of a shrug. "Half-naked." The heat was in her neck and her face now.

A grin slowly began to curve his lips.

"You think I'm good-looking?" he asked, terribly pleased with himself.

"I swear to God, Jason, if you make a big deal out of this, I'm going to go all *Game of Thrones* on you and stick my fingers in your eyes."

He grinned, clearly pleased with this turn in their profes-
sional relationship. "Okay, Cersei. Well now that the cat is
out of the bag, I think you're pretty good-looking too. So now
that we know the landscape…"

"Stop, Jason. We should never have gone down that
path."

He didn't agree or disagree, but held up the bottle of
whisky again. "How about that drink?"

"I don't really drink whisky. But I'd like a double."

Jason laughed. He was still grinning when he turned away
from her to get a highball glass. He returned to the table and
set the glass before her, still grinning, still far too pleased
with himself, his hazel eyes twinkling with delight at this turn
of events.

She ignored him. She was very good in her ability to
ignore him and trusted she would not falter this time. "Thank
you," she said, and sipped the whisky. It burned along with
her pride as it went down her throat.

"Sip it. It's not water," he advised, and tapped his glass to
hers. "Isn't it funny how you think you know someone and
discover you don't know them at all?"

"You're making a big deal out of it! I don't know
anything about you," she said hoarsely.

"Except that I'm good-looking. And apparently unsettling
in a half-naked state."

"And full of yourself, too," she said with a bit of a smile.

He grinned. "You actually know a lot about me,
Mallory. More than I know about you, apparently." He
winked at her.

"I really don't. I mean, I know you're a workaholic.
Everyone in Hollywood knows that. And you tend to date for
about a month before you move on."

"Before *they* move on," he corrected her, and with a twirl

of his fingers, he added, "Because of the workaholic thing. What else do you know?"

"That you have a big summerhouse in Maine. And that you are ridiculously unorganized. But that's about it."

"Okay, what would you like to know about me? I'm an open book." He gestured with his fork. "Go ahead. Ask."

"I didn't know you'd lost your parents at a young age." Mallory sipped again. "You sort of dropped that on me this morning. I can't imagine how devastating."

"Don't try—it's not fun," he said, and glanced up at another peal of thunder and a bolt of lightning.

"I'm sorry," she said. "I was surprised by it, that's all. You said a plane crash?"

"Yeah," Jason said. He glanced away from her. "My dad was flying. They were headed north to pick up my older brother Phillip, and there was bad weather." He shook his head. "It was so long ago." He looked into his glass, then picked up the bottle and poured a little more whisky into it.

"What happened afterward? Where did you go?"

"My uncle Graham and aunt Claire took us in. We lived with our cousins. Four of them, three of us."

"Wow," Mallory said softly. "That's a lot of kids." She knew a little about a lot of kids. There had been five in her family.

"All boys."

"*Seven*? That's a KPOP boy band."

Jason laughed. "I'll let you in on a secret. The accident, and the combining of families, is why I'm so in to film."

"Really?" This was interesting—she'd assumed he'd gotten into the film industry in the usual way—through family or business connections.

"Yep. Movies and television provided an escape for me after the shock of losing my parents. And there were suddenly seven of us. It was a lot to handle at my age. I had so many questions that went unanswered." He paused a moment and shook his head. "So I escaped. I'd come home from school and go to my room and lock myself in with movies. Every movie I could get my hands on. Classics like *Casablanca* and *Gone with the Wind*. Fringe movies like *Dazed and Confused* or blockbusters like *Jaws*—you get the picture. And when you watch movies back to back, over and over again, you start to get a sense of story arc, and how to construct the arc and how to pace it through several scenes. Because when those things don't work, you notice."

"That is definitely self-taught," Mallory said. She was impressed—how astute he must have been as a teen.

"Yep. I escaped into that world, and when the movies I watched finally numbed the pain, I decided I wanted to be a part of it. I worked my ass off to get a scholarship to the USC film school."

Mallory tried not to look as astounded as she felt. She and Inez had guessed he'd come from some privileged background where he was lauded for every achievement and his path greased into the finest schools. She could not have guessed that his interest in art had come from a place of such pain.

She definitely could not have guessed he'd attended USC on a *scholarship*.

"What about you?" Jason asked as he cleaned his plate and pushed it aside. "I don't know much about you either, other than you are very by the book."

"That's not true." She laughed.

"It's true and you know it. Where are your parents?"

"Oh. Pomona," she said with a flick of her wrist. Her life was definitely not as interesting as his had been.

"Pomona. Where is that?"

"It's a Los Angeles suburb. There's not much going on there, to be honest." That was an understatement.

"Okay," he said, and picked up his glass of whisky. "Tell me."

Honestly, Mallory felt that her parents were topics that were better left in a closet somewhere. They were children of the seventies. Products, her dad had once said, of the California hippie culture. They'd met at a pollution protest. Their marriage was not a legal one—they'd written their own vows and said them to each other under a Joshua tree. In the picture, her dad had worn his hair in a ponytail, and her mother's hair had hung long and free and untrimmed. They'd never changed their look—they still wore their hair in that way, except that her dad's ponytail was silver now, and her mother's hair was frizzy and streaked with gray. But at least she'd stopped wearing the flower crowns somewhere along the way.

Her parents were hard to explain. "My family is different," she said.

"Well thanks, but that is really vague. Everyone's family is different."

"Okay. My parents were hippies when they met. Last of a dying breed." Another clap of thunder overhead caused her to pick up her glass and sip more. "They went with the live-and-let-live theory of parenting."

Jason gave her a funny smile. "What does that mean?"

"It means that there were no rules and no boundaries." Her parents had been social warriors all of her life, tackling the issues of the day and dragging their children along. They'd tried to instill into their large brood the need to have every person's voice heard. "You don't know how lucky you are to live in a country where you have the right to protest!" Mallory's father used to say, pounding the table with his fist to punctuate his passion for free speech or the injustices in the world.

For the first eleven years of her life, Mallory and her siblings had lived like forest sprites, flitting through life without any guidance whatsoever other than to look out for one another. Their task, their parents had explained, was to experience life as it came to them—not have experience dictated to them. That meant it they wanted to eat through a box of Count Chocula in one sitting, so be it—they would pay the consequences later when their bodies rebelled. If it meant walking out the door and racing across a busy thoroughfare to check out a dog behind a fence, they should do that, too. If they got hit by a car, they would remember to look both ways. If they didn't want to practice reading or writing, no problem—the desire would come soon enough, so their parents' thinking went. "You can't force a round peg into a square hole," her father would say.

Mallory had believed the entire world lived the same as they did, *free to be you and me*, so to speak, in a small, three-bedroom house. They ate ramen with ketchup when the rent was late. They read by candle when the lights were turned off. They built small campfires and slept in tents when they were evicted.

"Sounds kind of cool," Jason ventured.

"Not so much. Kids need boundaries and rules. Mom and Dad treated us like experiments."

"Weird thing to say, but I am intrigued," Jason said with a laugh. "Like how?"

"We were a merry band of Pippy Longstockings, to be honest. We were homeschooled, which, in practice, meant that on the days we wanted to learn something, we could. On the days we didn't feel like it, we didn't. You can imagine how often we didn't feel like it. We had no boundaries, we were free to come and go as we liked. We had no televisions, only books."

It felt so strange to be talking about this now. That life had been so long ago, and she'd changed so much. She recognized that her life had made her who she was today, and without that life, she probably wouldn't be as driven as she was now. She didn't like to recall it. People could be so judgmental.

"But you went to college," Jason said.

"I did. I really wanted to go." Her siblings hadn't gone, even with her begging them to apply themselves, to go to school, to have a better life than the one they'd had growing up. Today, Meghan was an accounting clerk at an electrical company. Edison was seriously overweight, no thanks to the Count Chocula habit he still had, and was a maintenance worker at a local elementary school. Nadia was married with four kids and pregnant with her fifth. And Jet? Mallory's oldest brother was eighteen when he headed out to join the Navy against his parents' wishes. "You're feeding a war machine, Jet," his father had pleaded with him. "We've taught you to love peace."

"The pay is pretty good, Dad, and I'll get to go on a ship," Jet had said. And off he'd gone, disappearing into the world. They heard from him from time to time, but mostly, Jet had left that life behind.

"So you just decided to go to college?" Jason asked.

"In a way, yeah," she said.

"Tell me," he said, and he seemed genuinely interested.

"You don't know what it's like, to brought up like that. We were unkempt and uneducated. We all wore our hair long, like our parents. We looked like swamp creatures, too, because we only bathed when we wanted to. We dressed in hand-me-down clothes my parents picked up at local church bazaars and garage sales. We were required to volunteer two hours a week at the local soup kitchen and then had to spend so many weekends protesting inequalities with all these other, like-minded people."

"Ah," Jason said.

"But one thing they did was take us to the library every week. I suspect because it had air-conditioning, but still. We went every week. That's where I discovered television and movies. On Saturdays, they had cartoons in one room. And you could rent movies. By the time I was eleven, my parents finally had to face the fact that at least one of them needed a job, because feeding five kids and two dogs was too much for them to handle. My dad took a job in Los Angeles, which was quite the commute. My mom took a job in a grocery store. And we all went to school for the first time. But that's where I found my people. My organized, ambitious people."

"Okay, I'm starting to form a picture," Jason said, smiling.

"All that time, not five blocks from my house, was this amazing world of schedules and organization and boundaries." She laughed. "There was none of the "find your own boundaries" there, because the boundaries were clearly demarcated." She'd learned of all the myriad possibilities of adult occupations, whereas before, she assumed the world of jobs existed around cashiers and delivery vans or no job at all, like her parents. There were three-ring binders with brightly colored tabs, and that one could sort out her entire life into one of them. More, if she liked.

"Let me guess—you were the teacher's pet."

"And straight-A student," Mallory said proudly. "I really loved hearing about my potential. Oh, and I could hang out after school and watch movies in my history teacher's class. I think he knew I was struggling to keep my foot in that world, you know?"

"At least you had someone who noticed it. In my case, I was one of seven. Not the oldest, not the youngest, but just in the middle and I never felt as if anyone cared what I did. Except my cousin, Ross. He was a middle kid, too. He would come watch movies with me." He looked down a moment, as if remembering. "So you discovered your love of three-ring binders in elementary school, and then what?"

"Then?" She snorted. "Then I began to organize the lives for my siblings. They are younger than me, except for Jet. But they needed help getting to school and staying focused, and I took that job on."

Jason laughed. "You really seem to like organizing other people's lives."

"I do. But some people's lives need a lot of organizing. Anyway, I drifted further and further away from my parents' ideals and found my own. I discovered I wanted to achieve things with my life. I wanted to explore the world I saw in films and the stories I told myself," she said, gesturing to her head. "I figured no one was going to do it for me."

She remembered that years after she'd left home, Mallory's sister Meghan had once suggested that the reason Mallory wore her blonde hair in a short bob was because it was the exact opposite style of her mother and father. "That's not why," Mallory had scoffed. "I wear it this way because it's so easy to take care of." But the truth was closer to Meghan's theory. Mallory had never really thought of it until then, but even she could see that everything she did was the opposite of what her parents would do. Plus, it was a stylish cut. Her mother was not stylish. Her mother would point out that the desire to *be* stylish was not a proletariat virtue and was the very definition of vanity.

Mallory was okay with a little bit of vanity. She liked being stylish and frankly, it was hard not to want to be stylish when one worked in Hollywood. She'd discovered that the hard way when she'd graduated from college with a degree in theater arts from Chapman University and had started pounding the pavement in search of acting gigs. One casting director told her she looked like she was a receptionist at a third-rate hair salon. Needless to say, she didn't get the part. So yes, she'd become a little more interested in style and her physical appearance since leaving home.

"For the record," Jason said, "I am really glad you discovered you wanted to organize people's lives and tell stories, because I don't know what I'd do without you."

Mallory smiled with surprise. "Wow. That might be the nicest thing you ever said to me."

"You have a remarkable story, Mal. I'm a little embarrassed I never asked more about your life. I'm a little in awe of you right now."

"Please," she said, with a flick of her wrist. "I survived, that's all. Like anyone would."

"Not just anyone. Some of us really struggled to survive. Some of us had every advantage a rich white boy can have and still struggled."

"You're comparing apples to oranges. I didn't lose my parents."

"Not permanently...but it sounds like in a way, you did. Sounds like we were both without that guidance. Sounds like we both used film to escape."

"Yeah," she said quietly. He was right—they'd been two kids missing the umbrella of parents over their lives.

Jason took a drink, then stood up, and picked up the plates. "Want some dessert? I think there is some pie in the fridge."

"No thanks." Mallory looked at the window. The rain was still coming down in sheets, but not as hard as in the beginning. It was cozy, and the whisky, while not her thing, was warming her. How odd that their lives, at opposite ends of the economic spectrum, were so similar.

She wasn't mad at him anymore. She was glad she knew these things about him.

She also felt loose and warm, and while she felt this connection to him, he was still her boss. She looked at Jason's broad back. "So are you going to tell me about these changes to the schedule?"

"I won't lie, I'm a little afraid," he said, and turned around, grinning at her. "It was a hatchet job that will probably throw everything out of whack. But Cass was insistent we get some of the shoots out of the way that didn't require a lead actor. That's our first order of business—we have to find a new star."

He came back to the table with the bottle of whisky. Thunder rumbled again, but farther away. "You want to get comfortable first?"

Mallory blinked. "Excuse me?"

"I mean, settle in. The casting agency sent a link to some possibilities to replace Darien. I thought you might want to shower and change before we start to work."

She didn't know how she was going to settle in to her T-shirt and boxer shorts she normally wore to bed, but she could do with getting her bra off and a hot shower. She looked again to the window and the storm still raging around them. "You're sure it's okay if I stay here?"

Jason's smile was dazzling. He leaned over her to pick up the bottle of whisky. "I'm sure. But I have one condition."

"Lay it on me."

A spark appeared in his eye. "If you have too much

whisky and decide to make a pass at me, you promise to tell me it's happening so I'm not confused."

Mallory's belly did a funny little flip. But she rolled her eyes. "I'm so not going to make a pass at you, Jason."

"Famous last words." He moved away from her.

"Oh my God, it's true—you think you're such a stud."

"Hey, I wasn't the one freaked out by my lack of shirt. Come on, I'll show you to your room."

"You have to admit, that's not the way people meet their assistant at the door," she said as she grabbed her backpack and followed him.

"My assistant was supposed to call me. That way, I could put on a shirt and come and get her off the back drive." He picked up her suitcase and started up a wide staircase.

"Your assistant tried, but you didn't give her even a minute to get to a place where she could pick up a signal."

Jason led her down another wide, carpeted hallway. "My assistant is slow." He paused at a door and looked back, smiling as he opened it.

Mallory walked into the room before him. A little gasp of wonder escaped her lips. So *this* was how the other half lived. The room was beautiful, with an en suite bathroom, a big, four-poster bed, and most importantly, a view of the ocean and the storm raging over it. "Oh my God, Jason. This is *gorgeous*. Is this your room?"

"Nope. This is a guest room." He put her suitcase on a luggage rack. "I'm going to grab a shower, too. I'll meet you downstairs?" He smiled at her again. He'd smiled at her more tonight than he had the whole year she'd worked for him.

So Mallory smiled back, and it felt as if their smiles crossed and hung in the air between them. "Thanks, Jason."

"Yep." He paused at the door, his hand on the handle.

"Mallory…I'm really glad you're here." He went out, closing the door behind him.

Mallory turned a slow circle, taking in the room, then fell onto her back on top of the bed. She felt like Elizabeth Bennet must have felt when she finally saw Pemberly in *Pride and Prejudice*.

She was really glad she was here, too.

CHAPTER SEVEN

CLEANED AND SHOWERED AND PROPERLY DRESSED FOR Mallory's sake, Jason pushed aside some files on the kitchen table, opened his laptop, and pulled up the headshots the casting agency had sent him.

Mallory appeared a few minutes later looking refreshed. She was wearing yoga pants that fit her almost too well, and a plain white T-shirt beneath a gray hoodie. Her hair, still wet, was slicked back behind her ears. She smiled sheepishly at him. "Wow, look at you. You have on a shirt."

"Anything to make your stay more enjoyable. Come take a look."

He'd pulled a pair of chairs around so they would view the files together. He had also refreshed her drink. If she noticed, she didn't say anything.

Mallory took a seat next to him, picked up the drink, and sipped. "Whisky is growing on me," she said. "Okay, what have we got?"

"A dozen headshots of actors who are currently available. I want to get a couple of them in to read for the part right away. We start shooting in a little over a week."

He pulled up the first headshot. A young blond man stared thoughtfully back at them. "Too young," he said instantly.

"Too pretty," Mallory said.

The next one had potential. Mallory leaned forward a little to study him, her head near Jason's. She smelled sweet, like flowers. Like the sort of bouquet he would send to a woman to make up for some sin.

Mallory tapped through to some different shots of the man. She wrinkled her nose. "I don't know. He's got a dad bod."

"What?" Jason turned his attention away from the study of her delicate ear. "No he doesn't. He looks good."

"Trust me. No one wants the object of their fantasy to have even the hint of a gut. This is the lead, you know. The character all the woman should fall for, and he can't have a dad bod."

Jason looked down at his belly.

Without even looking at him, Mallory said, "You're not starring in a show. And you don't have a dad bod."

How did she do that? He clicked on the next one. "How about this guy?"

Mallory cocked her head to one side and studied him. "He has possibilities. But he looks a little effeminate in the chin, don't you think?"

"No." He looked like a regular guy to Jason.

"Seriously, look at him," she said, nodding. She picked up her whisky and sipped. "There is nothing wrong with his looks, but he doesn't look hard enough for this role. We need someone grizzled."

Jason laughed. "Have you ever met Darien Simmons?" he joked. "He has never looked grizzled a day in his life. He looks like he's just finished afternoon tea."

"I always thought his look was wrong for the role, you

know? *Bad Intentions* is so gritty. More *True Detective* than *Pink Panther*. Imagine if we had someone like Woody Harrelson or Russell Crowe in the role."

Interesting she would say that. When they'd done the original casting for the show, before Mallory had come on board, he and Cass had decided that a more sophisticated actor was better for the part. Frankly, Cass had been insistent and Jason had bowed to his experience. But he saw Mallory's point.

He flipped to the next actor. This one had a scruff of a beard and lines around his eyes. A true character actor, fully weathered. He looked to be in his fifties. "What about him?"

She was already shaking her head. "Cheekbones aren't right."

"*Cheekbones?*"

"I mean, he's fine in real life, but for this show, we need defined cheekbones. There was this whole study done on the facial features people respond to." She spared him a look from the corner of her eye. "Didn't you read it? I put it on your desk."

"No, I didn't read it," he said, mocking her voice.

Mallory smiled pertly.

"Come on, his cheekbones are fine," Jason said, and resisted the urge to touch his own chin. "Makeup can build that up."

"I qualified it. I said not in real life." She smiled at him. "You're taking this too personally. You have perfect cheekbones."

He rolled his eyes. "We're not talking about me."

"Don't feel bad, Jason. It's natural to compare yourself to the actors."

He gave her a withering look. "I don't compare myself to the actors," he said, trying to sound bored.

"Everyone does."

"Next," Jason said. He was not going to discuss how he compared himself to every actor on set. It was impossible not to. There were men in this world who were unbelievably fit and handsome. It was astounding, really. He realized Mallory wasn't moving and glanced at her.

Her eyes were sparkling with delight. She was loving this. And when she looked at him like that, he loved it, too. More than he should.

"Here's one," Jason said, forcing his attention back to the screen. The man had curly hair, crinkles around the eyes, and a wry smile.

"Now there is a man with sex appeal." Mallory jotted down his name, then took another sip of her drink. "He *oozes* sex appeal."

Jason looked at the picture again and shook his head. He wasn't getting it. "What is sex appeal, anyway?"

"You know."

"Not really. Explain it to me."

Mallory took another sip of her drink. "Sex appeal is…" She took another sip, then twisted around in her seat. "It's attitude. Confidence. And it's the way he looks at you, you know? Like he could have you if he wanted, and you know that he could."

Jason looked at the actor's headshot. That guy could have them if he wanted?

"It's also a deep voice and a masculine frame." She wasn't looking at Jason or the headshot. She was looking at the window. "It's all of those things. Sex appeal, to me, is a man who has power and desire…but wrapped into a package that makes you feel safe." She looked at Jason again. "Like Russell Crowe."

"Russell Crowe is the standard of sex appeal now?"

"He's an example." Mallory leaned forward and looked at the man on the screen. "Yep. This guy has it. We should bring him in."

"So where were you when we did the original casting?" Jason asked as they began to scroll in search of a second candidate.

"I was about to take a job as a clerk in a tax office." She smiled at him from the corner of her eye. "But if I'd been working for you, I'm sure I would have been manning the phones."

Jason smiled. "Probably so. I'm sure I wouldn't have believed you knew anything, much less the mysteries of sex appeal."

"Even after my interview?" Mallory laughed. "I was pretty proud of myself that day. I got my act together in a couple of hours and nailed it." She gave a little fist pump.

Jason smiled. He remembered her interview. He'd been desperate to fill a slot after Holly had quit in a flurry of tears and a list of disappointments with him. His disorganization had struck again. "All I remember is that you seemed competent."

"I seemed competent? That's it? That's all you remember?"

"I remember you had your binder. Does that count?"

"Jason!" she said loudly, and picked up her whisky again, sloshing a drop onto the table. "You really don't remember? I told you I wanted to be a director. We talked about making films."

"Yeah, well, everyone who comes through that door wants to be a filmmaker or an actor."

"Well, I meant it. I want to be a director. I'm working on my own short films."

"You are?" Jason pulled up another headshot of a man

who was so crusty looking, it was surprising he wasn't holding a giant fish aloft.

"I am. I was working on it this week while you were away. It's a short film about a woman who goes to get milk out of her fridge, and the carton is empty, and she goes into a murderous rage because it's the final straw with her roommate, and she kills her. But then realizes what she's done and has to dispose of the body and cover her crime." She went on to explain the plot in a little more detail, and how the woman's life was unraveling, and how in the end, the viewer would think she'd gotten it together, but the film ended with her going to the fridge and finding another empty milk carton, and we realize it wasn't the roommate at all—the woman had lost her mind. She was animated—she had a passion for this project, which didn't surprise him. He understood what it felt like when a story was clicking along and all the parts were fitting together.

"I'm almost done," Mallory said. "I'm submitting it to a contest."

No wonder she didn't want to come to Maine. Mallory didn't do anything halfway and she never left anything unfinished. "It sounds great," Jason said. "I'd love to see it."

She gave him a pert little smile that made him feel a little buzzy inside. "I'd love to show you when I'm done. I think it's really good. I've got three more scenes to shoot, and then of course it needs to be edited. This guy won't work, by the way."

It took Jason a second to realize she was talking about a headshot. He'd been captivated by her energy and smile.

"But this guy will." She clicked on another photo. The man looked like an unkempt and older version of Keanu Reeves. Even Jason could see the sex appeal in this guy. He could also see him in the role of detective.

"Yeah," Jason said, nodding. "He looks good. Call Audrey in the morning and have her get these two guys out here at once. Fly them in."

Mallory jotted down a note. "And then what?"

"And then, we call Cass and finalize two locations we've been a little iffy about. We have to be ready to go in a little more than a week."

Mallory turned in her chair so she was facing him. "So how long am I going to be here?"

"Two days, tops," Jason said without thinking. "Just help me get a new lead and the last two locations nailed down. Sound good?"

Mallory looked out the window again as if she was pondering this. The rain was light now, the storm flashing brilliantly over the ocean. "Two days," she repeated, which he took as agreement. "But I want to move to a hotel." She slid her gaze back to him.

"Absolutely," he said. "Me, too. It's easier to be near Cass and the crew."

"Okay, then," she said. She sipped more of the whisky, then stood up, stumbling a little as she attempted to step away from the table. She laughed. "Uh-oh. I broke my cardinal rule and drank on the job."

"Uh-oh," he said with a chuckle. "I think you're safe. There were mitigating circumstances."

"Riiiight," she said playfully. "But you know something Jason?" she asked as she swayed into the kitchen. "Tonight wasn't as miserable as I thought it was going to be."

He choked on a laugh of surprise. "Umm...thank you? So I make you miserable?" He got up and followed her into the kitchen.

"Well, sometimes. I mean, you're my boss. Bosses exist to make people miserable." She glanced up at him, and her eyes were sparkling in a way that made him sparkle, too. Mallory was so appealing to him. She wasn't as beautiful as women he'd met in the industry, but she was pretty. And there was so much more to her appeal than her good looks. She was giggling at him. "Oh, I made you sad. I didn't mean to make you sad. You shouldn't listen to me, anyway, because I think I'm a little drunk."

"I think you are, too," he said, and tucked a tress of her blonde hair behind her ear.

"It's your fault. Are you maybe a little drunk?"

"I'm feeling pretty good." He was not a little drunk on anything but lust, he feared. The woman turned him on.

She turned on the faucet and reached for the plates, brushing against him. "Oops," she said when she'd done it a third time.

"Let's leave it until morning," Jason suggested. "I'm afraid you'll drop something."

"I'm not *that* drunk. I'm not the night of the dailies drunk." She paused a moment, her hand on the faucet. "That really happened, you know."

"Oh, I know."

She turned off the water and turned. "Hey, let me ask you something—did you *really* think you were responsible for what happened?"

"Yes."

"Really?" she asked, her eyes narrowing. "Because I don't see how you *could. have. missed. it.*" She poked him in the chest with each word.

She was feeling no pain, that was for sure. "Missed what?"

"That I really do have a massive crush on you." The minute she said it, she put her fingers to her lips. "Did I just say that?"

The sparkle in him was getting a little more intense. Maybe he'd had more to drink than he thought, because all he wanted to do right now was kiss her. "Yes you did. Which means I was *right*. You *do* have a thing for me."

"I shouldn't have said that. Now it's going to get all weird like it did the first time, isn't it?"

"Not with me," he said.

She smiled, her eyes bright behind her glasses. She swayed forward a little and he caught her by the elbow, righting her. She seemed not to notice. "So all and all, riding out the storm with you, which, you know, would be my worst nightmare, has been very interesting."

"You're not exactly helping with my self-confidence."

"Don't take it personally," she advised, and laid her hand on his chest. "Since I'm laying it all out here in a whisky-coated haze, you want to know something else?"

"Sure." He was smiling, because he suspected Mallory was going to regret this in the morning, particularly the part about having a crush on him. He hadn't believed her the night of the dailies. He'd chalked it up to their being drunk. But now that he knew she did, he figured she probably wouldn't make eye contact for a month.

"You have sex appeal, Jason Blackthorne." She arched a brow, as if she were pleased with her assessment, then pushed him, so he bounced up against the counter.

He couldn't suppress a chuckle. He was going to enjoy teasing her about this. "I don't think you should be telling me everything you're thinking right now."

"Don't tell me what to do," she said, and moved closer to him, so now Jason was trapped between her and the counter-top. "I have an idea, the perfect way to end this crazy day. Do you want to know what it is?"

"Honestly? I'm a little afraid to know."

She leaned closer, her gaze falling to his mouth. She was going to kiss him. Jason curled the fingers of one hand around the edge of the countertop, and put the other one on her arm, forcing her to lift her gaze from his mouth. "I think you might regret this in the morning, Mallory," he said softly.

"You always think you know everything," she murmured, and kissed him.

He'd seen it coming, but Jason was just as surprised as she was that night in his office. Mallory so straight and narrow, so rule oriented. Except when she'd had a little to drink. She slid her arms up his chest, rose up on her toes and pressed her soft, warm lips against his.

Jason instantly put his hands on her arms and pulled her away from his mouth. His heart was beginning to race. He didn't trust himself, didn't think he had enough strength to stop this. "I specifically asked you if you were going to make a pass at me to tell me so I wouldn't be confused."

"I forgot." She smiled. "I'm making a pass. A big one."

Jason's body was totally into the idea. But his head…his head kept whispering *Darien.* "Mallory, I just fired Darien—"

"I know, that was *awful.*" She grabbed his head in both her hands and pulled it down, kissing him again.

"I think you've lost your mind," he said against her lips.

"Maybe," she murmured back against his lips.

That was it, as much resistance as he could put up against her. Because maybe he had a bit of a crush on her, too. When her tongue began to tease his, he somehow managed to slide his hand up under her T-shirt and hoodie and find her breast. It was enough to fry his thoughts into nothing. Everything became instinct—he was moving, lifting her up on the countertop. She shoved her hands into his hair, pulling him closer, his body into hers. He didn't understand why it was always so charged between them, why it always felt like there were magnets pulling them together, but the flame had been lit in him, and the desire was torching him.

Mallory drew her knees up around him and pressed her body against his. He was ready to launch, ready to do the deed here where they stood. He was ready to make love to this woman in a way she would not soon forget. But that clanging thought about Darien in the back of his mind somehow pierced his thoughts. *What was he doing?*

Jason managed to get a grip of his emotions and the sensations rifling through him. He pressed his forehead to hers, wiped her bottom lip with the pad of his thumb. "This is not appropriate," he said roughly.

"That's what makes it so much fun," she said dreamily.

"We *work* together," he reminded her.

Mallory opened her eyes. "But we're not working right now," she said hopefully, and let go of his wrist that he hadn't even realized she was holding until that moment, so intent was he on the sensations running through his body. She wrapped her arms around his neck and kissed him again.

"Are you going to freeze me out tomorrow?" he asked as she put his hands on her waist.

"Don't know," she said, and nibbled at his bottom lip.

"This is *nuts*," Jason said, but lifted her off the counter anyway.

Mallory wrapped her legs around him as he began to carry them out of the kitchen. "It's totally nuts," she agreed. "But I can't help it. I like it so much, Jason. Don't you?"

Jason liked it more than he could say. "I like it," he said gruffly, and ignored the thought that he ought to be the strong one here, ought to put an end to things before they both did something they would regret. He clearly was not the strong one, because he kept walking, pausing only at the foot of the stairs to put her on her feet. They paused there for a moment and looked at each other. They didn't need words, Jason realized in a heady moment. Mallory was smiling. He was, too. He wrapped his hand around hers, squeezing lightly.

She squeezed back. "We're grownups. We can do what we want."

"Right," he said uncertainly. Because somewhere deep down, Jason knew that what was about to happen was not a game to him. It was a game changer. He was about to opening the door to a whole other universe, and he didn't know what was behind it or even if he wanted to go through. But the way she was looking at him, with all that desire swimming in her big blue eyes, with that adorably hopeful-yet-nervous little smile, made him feel about as sexy as he ever had in his life.

Actually, come to think of it, he hadn't felt sexy in a very long time.

"So?" she asked. "Do you want to go upstairs? Or do you want to talk about production schedules?"

Jason bit back a laugh. "That's no choice." He kissed her fingers, then wrapped his hand around hers, and lead her upstairs, making her take them two at a time.

CHAPTER EIGHT

Mallory didn't know how they got into his room, exactly, because the journey was pretty handsy and intense. But when she opened her eyes, she was in another room with a spectacular view of the ocean and a storm that was still lighting the horizon. There was nothing left of it on shore but a steady rain.

Jason turned away from her to shut the door. While he did, Mallory looked around the room. His clothes were draped across one of two upholstered chairs in the bay window. On top of a dresser she could see a wallet, some coins, his familiar watch and a pair of sunglasses. The door to the closet was standing open, and a duffel bag, a baseball bat, and what looked like hiking boots were on the floor.

This was his room, his summer sanctum, she guessed, and she was standing here because she'd confessed her huge crush and was at long last acting on it.

Correction—she would be acting on it just as soon as Jason stopped talking.

She slowly turned to face him, surprised by the number of words that were flowing out of his mouth. Was he nervous?

He sounded almost nervous. What did he have to be nervous about? He was so handsome, so sexy. He could be a cover model. She'd once said that to Inez, and Inez had punched Mallory in the arm and shouted at her to wake up.

Well, she was fully awake right now and horny, and she didn't want to talk. "Jason. Stop talking," she advised as she took him in, head to foot.

"What?" He shoved his hand through his hair. "Sorry. I was asking if we should establish some ground rules here."

"Ground rules?"

"I don't want things to be weird between us after…this."

"Stop it. You are totally ruining the moment," she said. Which wasn't really true—it would take at least two semi rigs to pull her out of this now. She just wanted him to talk less and kiss more.

"I am?"

"You worry too much. That's my job," she said, and put her arms around his neck.

"But you're not worrying, so I feel like I need to do it." Jason removed her glasses and put them aside. He smiled at her. "You are seriously cute with or without them, you know that?" He bent his head and kissed her, and an electric current shot through her.

"I have an idea," she said as he slid his hands up under her hoodie. "We get down first, then talk about it later."

He smiled lopsidedly. "Since when do you talk this way? Don't answer that." He kissed her, slow and easy, his lips moving on hers, his tongue tangling with hers. When he lifted his head, he kissed the bridge of her nose and said, "Let's get down."

Those words, spoken with his deep voice, shot the electric thrill into a nuclear category. Her fantasy, her forbidden pleasure, was *happening*, and she was so on board with it, she could captain this ship. Any qualms she'd had about the appropriateness of this had dissolved in the force of the storm, and she was going to go for broke. For once, she was not going to overthink it. She was going to shut out Inez's voice from her thoughts, and she was going to keep her hands and feet inside the box and ride this ride.

But she would have to get her bearings first, because Jason was kissing her fully, his tongue dipping between her lips, his touch warm and heavy. He put his arm around her waist and lowered her onto the bed, his knee between her legs, his body on top of hers. She pushed against him, trying to roll him onto his back, but Jason only intensified the kiss. Mallory leveraged him with her knee, finally succeeding in getting him on his back and then eagerly trying, but unsuccessfully, to take his T-shirt off him.

"Hold on," Jason said, holding his arms out. "Take it easy."

"No. I'm going for it."

He laughed. "Maybe we go for it at the same pace." He sat up, his hands on her rib cage. "Maybe we agree it's not a race to the finish." He kissed her collarbone. "Are you in a hurry?" He kissed the hollow of her throat. "I hope not, because I have some exploring I need to do."

Oh. She felt herself melting into his touch. "No," she said weakly.

Jason took her head in his hands and kissed her mouth in that way he had that made her insides turn to jelly. Not a moment later, Mallory was tumbling down the rabbit hole of want. Her idea of taking charge and bringing it to him began to slip and slide away. Jason was too good at this. He took off his shirt, guided her hands to his chest. And when she had dragged her fingers over his pecs and down to his waist, he slipped his hands under her hoodie and T-shirt, pulled them over her head, and lowered himself down to take her breast in his mouth.

So much for taking charge—Mallory was officially putty in his hands…and what big hands he had.

Jason slowly leaned backward, taking her with him, until he was flat on his back and she was stretched out on top of him. "How's this?" he asked as he grazed her earlobe.

"*This* is fantastic."

He suddenly moved, his arm anchoring her around the waist as he very acrobatically put her on her back beneath him. He smiled down at her and Mallory smiled at him. The way her body had heated and her breathing had shortened, she could tell she was in for the ride of a lifetime.

He put his hands on the waist of her yoga pants and started to inch them down. "Still good?" he purred.

"Still good," she answered breathlessly.

He pushed her pants down and off and tossed them on the floor. In the next moment, he was kicking off his shorts, and revealing how hard and eager he was for her. He braced himself over her so that he could kiss her neck at the point it curved into her shoulder.

"Get up here," she whispered, pulling on his thick biceps, urging him to move on top of her.

Jason grinned. "You're impatient."

"Yes."

"Okay then," he said, and moved up as he slipped his fingers in between her legs. "I'm here."

Mallory sucked in a breath and closed her eyes as he moved his fingers on her and in her. "This isn't fair. I really wanted to take the lead."

He leaned down and whispered in her ear, "*Next time.*" He rolled them again, putting her on top once more. Mallory's trip down the rabbit hole was now a fast and furious slide into oblivion, She felt like she was floating in a sea of pure sensation as she kissed him and his hands explored her. He moved them again, his lips now tracing a path down the middle of her body, following that trail with his hands. He dipped his tongue into the valley of her sex. It was an intoxicating, frothy concoction of skin and lips and desire all mixing into one utterly surreal experience. So deliciously earthy and with a promise of the ultimate satisfaction.

They swam along in their private sea, both of them reaching and stroking, kissing and sliding. It was foreplay and sex in a way Mallory had never quite experienced. It was twinkly and fiery, tender and fervent at the same time. The physical sensations churned with her emotions, truly rocking her world.

She was deep into that shimmering space when Jason suddenly sat up and groped around the nightstand next to the bed, producing a condom. A moment later, he pulled her into his body and slipped in between her legs. He paused, braced above her. He smiled appreciatively. Even fondly. "You have some pretty amazing sex appeal, too, Mallory Price. You're sexy as hell." And with that, he entered her, sliding slowly, giving her body time to accept him.

The pleasure of him inside her was exquisite. She pitched forward into it, pressing into every bit of his body she could reach or touch, seeking every bit of the sensation he was exciting in her. He caressed her as he moved, slow and fluid at first, his mouth on hers in one long, stupefyingly seductive kiss. He took his time with her, unwilling to rush the climax.

For Mallory, it was passionate agony. Her pulse beat so hard she could hear it pounding in her veins. Her body was straining for his like a divining rod, her thoughts so focused on reaching a climax it was a wonder she didn't implode. He began to quicken his stroke in a blur of touch and scent, of length and breadth, of breath and moans. She felt wild beneath him, an animal unleashed from its tether. She bit lightly into his shoulder, kissed his mouth, rocked against him in time to his own movements. She was fully ignited, her release building to a powerful conclusion. Jason muttered something incomprehensible, grabbed one of her hands and laced his fingers with hers, pressing it into the bed. He was moving quickly now with a maddening tempo, until Mallory let herself go with a groan of sexual gratification as her release crashed through her, washing out the months of pent-up desire for Jason Blackthorne.

Jason gave in, too, thrusting powerfully into her one last time with a moan against her shoulder.

Mallory felt dazed by it all. It was several moments before she was capable of the slightest movement except breathing. It seemed decades passed before Jason's voice woke her from the fog. "God, Mallory." He lifted his head and gazed at her with such an unfathomable expression that her heart raced—she felt the emotions in her that she was seeing in him. Satisfaction, a bit of surprise, more than a little affection.

Was it really possible that Jason had affection for her?

She had affection for him. It was hammering away in her chest and curling into a smile on her lips. This was so wrong on so many levels, but Mallory didn't care.

She was bewitched.

"If I knew you were going to turn me on like that, I would have brought you to Maine a long time ago," he said, and kissed her cheek.

"If I knew you were going to turn me on like that, I wouldn't have come," she said honestly.

Jason laughed. "Well, baby, the cat is out of the bag." He dislodged himself from her body, gathered her in his arms, and rolled onto his back, bringing her along to nestle in his side.

Mallory didn't want to think about any cats or bags right now. She felt exhilarated and happy. And a little like a sex goddess. This gorgeous man was telling her that she turned him on, and it made her feel vibrant and sexy and very happy to have another go at it.

Jason's smile deepened as he looked at her. "You're beautiful."

She laughed. "You're buttering me up again. You probably have some insane task you want me to do."

He smiled, cupped her chin. "I just want you to be here with me in this moment."

Her smile went deeper. She had a drop-dead sexy man smiling at her and telling her she was beautiful and that he wanted her here, and there was no place she wanted to be.

She would think about the consequences tomorrow. Right now, she wanted only to feel this magnificent.

Jason gave her a funny smile and pushed her bangs from her face. "What are you thinking about?"

"That I want to do it again."

He laughed. "What are you waiting for?" He cupped her face and kissed her.

Mallory sank into him.

She was bewitched, all right.

CHAPTER NINE

THE SOUND OF THE PHONE RINGING SOMEWHERE FAR AWAY woke Jason. He opened his eyes and blinked, as the memory of last night came back to him in a rush.

He turned his head, smiling…but Mallory was not where he'd last seen her.

He sat up and looked around the room. The bathroom door was open and her clothes were gone. She hadn't pulled a disappearing act on him, had she?

He got out of bed and quickly dressed, then headed down-stairs in search of Mallory and his phone.

He heard his phone ring again and sprinted for the kitchen, grabbing it up off the bar on the fourth ring. He looked at the screen, saw several missed calls, then swiped to take the call. "Cass," he said, suppressing a yawn.

"This business with Darien is a fucking disaster," Cass announced gruffly. "It's hampering my creative flow and I don't like it."

It was hampering everyone's flow, obviously. "We're sorting it out," Jason said patiently. "We can talk about it when we go out today—"

"I'm not going," Cass said.

Jason suppressed a groan. "Cass." The man could be a royal pain in the ass when things weren't going to plan. Which, interestingly, they rarely did when making a series, which he would have assumed Cass would have learned that along the way. One had to be nimble and adjust, and one would think a veteran direction would know that. "We have to nail down those locations today. We need to get the lease agreements done."

"Which do you want, Jason? A location and a director who can't even think? Or a director who has had the time to work through the story structure in the middle of all this chaos? Do you want to be responsible for disrupting my creative flow?"

God forbid anyone touch Cass's *creative flow*. "Cass, be reasonable—"

"I'm being *hounded* by this Darien Simmons business! My manager has been inundated with calls wanting my comment. How is a man supposed to work? I should never have signed on for this."

"Whoa," Jason said. "What the hell is that supposed to mean?"

"I said what I said," Cass said. "I'm not going today and you need to get these reporters off my ass."

Jason had the thought he ought to check in with Marlene, his publicist in L.A. There was no telling how many calls he'd missed last night—but he'd been too caught up in Mallory.

Mallory. Where was she?

"Are you *hearing* me?" Cass roared in his ear.

"Jesus, Cass. *Yes*," he said. He hadn't heard, but it didn't matter. Among his other trying qualities, Cass also tended to repeat himself like someone's grandpa.

"If you could kindly handle this fucking debacle, it would be greatly appreciated," Cass snapped.

What did Cass think he was doing? Hanging around the pool? Going down to the club for a doubles match? "I *am*, Cass," Jason said firmly.

"Thank you," Cass said, and clicked off.

Jason tossed his phone onto the kitchen bar.

"Who was that?"

Jason turned around as Mallory walked into the kitchen. She'd showered and changed, and was wearing a blue pantsuit that reminded him a little of something a prosecutor would wear to court. She looked rested and happy.

"That was Cass." He didn't know if he should do it, but Jason put his hand on her waist and leaned forward, kissing her cheek.

Mallory smiled but stepped away from him, walking to the kitchen table and his temporary office. Jason didn't like anyone touching his things—a successful state of disorganization required a certain level of disorganization to be maintained. It was, in effect, his way or organizing himself. Mallory was the only one he allowed to touch his things. Somehow, she knew how to straighten it all out without making it worse for him.

"What did he want?" she asked.

"To get his creative flow back, which he says has been grossly affected by the Darien Simmons crisis."

Mallory pursed her lips.

"What?"

"Nothing."

"It's something, I can tell by looking at you. Say it."

She gave him a tentative smile. "As a matter of fact, I've been wanting to mention a few things. That is, if you don't mind hearing them."

Jason sighed softly. He appreciated her enthusiasm for the project, but they were in a bit of a crunch right now. It felt like the whole project was in revolt against him. "What things?"

Mallory squared her shoulders as if she was about to impart some devastating news, like his pet rabbit had died. She withdrew a piece of paper from her pocket and opened it. Great. She had a list. "I think there are some things we could do better. Like reduce the clunky transitions between scenes. Enhance the lighting in others—the series is gritty, but it's so dark you can hardly see it. There have been many instances in previous episodes, which I've documented, that could be vastly improved with better cinematography. Our director of photography is top notch, you know, but Cass doesn't always agree with him."

This was not news. Everyone knew that Cass and the DP, Neil Tarrelli, disagreed quite frequently, and usually loudly. Jason nodded, but he wasn't going to engage in review of the series right now—he was scrolling through his messages and the mess Darien had created. "Maybe so," he said. "But right now, we have to focus on getting some actors out here to audition and the last two locations locked down. Can you get them out here as soon as possible? Today would be preferred. Tomorrow will work."

When Mallory didn't answer, Jason looked up from his phone. "What?"

"Of course I can get them in." She turned away from him.

Was this the moment that the wonder of last night would make things weird? He had no one to blame but himself. "Fly them into Boston. We'll do the auditions at Blackstone Enterprises offices in the Hancock Tower. Fifty-third floor." He picked up his phone. "I'll call and let them know we need a conference room, but first I need to call

Marlene. Reporters are asking for interviews. Apparently, Darien is saying he didn't do anything and was fired unjustly, so we'll need to make a statement. Actually, get the lawyer on the phone for me," he said, pointing at Mallory's phone. He sat down at the kitchen table and opened his laptop.

"Right away," Mallory said in that cool manner she had at work, and just like that, they had slid back into their roles. As if last night hadn't happened. That was not how Jason wanted it to go. Last night *had* happened, and he wanted to talk to her about it. But now was not the time—there were too many fires to be stamped out first. He knew she understood that.

Mallory got the law firm on the phone for him, then picked up her phone and began making calls to arrange to fly the two actors to Boston to audition.

By noon, she'd gotten both actors on board and had arranged for a plane to bring one to Boston later today—the other would be coming from New York—and set the audition for tomorrow. Jason had talked to their lawyer, and the firm was drafting a statement concerning Darien. Marlene, their staff publicist, had the spin control in full gear.

"Okay," Jason said. "Next up, we lock down the last two locations. I'll get dressed and we'll go have a look."

"What about Cass?"

"He's not going," Jason said. "But I've got to get them locked in. So you're coming with me. If we need any special permissions, you can tackle that after the auditions."

"*Wait*, Jason," Mallory said, throwing up a hand. "Just how long am I going to be here? You said you needed help with casting."

Given last night, he would have thought—or hoped—that she'd want to stay on, at least for a little while. "A couple of days?"

She lowered her hand and stared at the floor, as if she was considering it. "I have to get a room first. I can't stay here."

"Wow," he said softly.

"Last night notwithstanding," she quickly amended. "But I can't stay in your family's house. It's not right. It's…it's uncomfortable."

He folded his arms and studied her. "Interesting perspective. Last night notwithstanding and all," he said, a bit peevishly. "But fine, Mallory. We'll stop at the Bickmore on the way." He smiled at her, and as he moved past her, he tangled his fingers with hers.

He knew they needed to talk. They needed to address the physical attraction between them, because he was not going to let it suffocate under their neglect this time. But the talk would just have to wait.

CHAPTER TEN

IF MALLORY COULD CHANGE ONE THING, IT WOULD BE HOW messy Jason could be. He left a trail wherever he went. She would have to resist the urge to clean up after him—at least stack the papers strewn across half the kitchen table. Because she was not going to add insult to the injury of having confessed her crush to him.

But then again, Mallory could be a little obsessive about having a neat workspace, as anyone at Blackthorne Entertainment could tell you. Still, she shuddered when she thought of what Inez would say if she knew Mallory had flown to Maine, to Jason's mansion, to confess she had a crush, and then spend the night with him, and then clean up after him. She would deserve every word of it, too.

But she couldn't help herself. By the time Jason came downstairs again, shaved and dressed for the day in jeans and a T-shirt, a sweater and sneakers, and looking certifiably delectable, she had cleaned up his little office space on the kitchen table. Just in time, too. Pam, who'd brought the risotto last night, had arrived with a cheerful wave, ready to tackle some housecleaning. Mallory would have died if she'd seen how the kitchen table looked.

"Beautiful day, isn't it?" Pam had asked.

It was gorgeous. The storm had left in its wake a cobalt-blue sky. Rain droplets attached to the leaves of the trees glistened like crystals in the sun. There were sailboats on the ocean, serenely moving along the surface. "It's paradise," Mallory agreed.

"Where are you from?"

"California. But I rarely see the ocean, if you can believe it. Seems like I'm always going the other way."

"Good morning, Pam," Jason said as he'd sauntered into the kitchen. He glanced around at Mallory's bags stacked neatly against one wall, then looked at her.

"Good morning, Jason!" Pam said cheerfully. "Did you weather the storm all right?"

"Like a boss," he said, and winked at Mallory. "How is Nana?"

"Oh, you know your grandmother. She's out inspecting for any damage in her garden. How long will you stay, Mallory?" Pam asked as she began to run water in the sink.

"Oh, I'm heading back to L.A. tomorrow."

"Maybe not that soon," Jason said.

"Probably," she countered, and shrugged lightly at his pointed look. She would decide when she left, thank you.

"We should go," he said, looking at his watch. He smiled at Pam. "Thanks for everything. The risotto was delicious. Just so you know, I'm getting a room in King Harbor. It will be easier for me to be close to the crew." He picked up some things from the table and ignored Mallory's studious look. "I'll come back later and get some things and check in on Nana."

He handed a notebook to Mallory, then bent down to pick up her things. "Ready?"

"Of course," she said pertly. She smiled at Pam. "Thanks again for everything."

"Take care, Mallory!" Pam called in a sing-song voice as they went out of the kitchen.

Mallory followed Jason out the front door and onto a drive. He popped the hatch of a Range Rover.

"Whose car is this?"

"It belongs to the estate," he said, and tossed her bags inside, closed it, turned around to her and said, "So you just decided you were flying back to L.A. tomorrow?"

"I did."

"I didn't give you permission."

"You're not the boss of me, Jason."

He arched a brow.

"Okay, *technically*, you are the boss of me. But only up to a certain point. I can't just leave L.A. without a return date. I have a life there you know." She got in the car and refused to look at him.

He marched around the driver's side, climbed in, started the car and looked at her. "I knew this would happen."

"Knew what would happen?"

"That you'd get verklempt and start acting weird. That's exactly what you did the last time."

He put the car in gear and started driving.

"*I'm* acting weird? You started barking orders at me first thing."

"I wasn't barking."

"You *barked*. And I didn't act *weird* the last time. I acted responsibly."

"Uh-uh, you're not getting away with that persnickety superiority thing with me. You were totally weird and you know it. You half admitted it last night. I'm sorry if I barked, but we have a bit of a crisis on our hands. I'm a little caught up in it and I can't totally change my personality just because we have insane sexual chemistry."

Mallory couldn't help but smile a little. They *did* have insane sexual chemistry, and she was glad to know it wasn't just her who thought so. Frankly, if she could, she would crawl onto his lap right now and kiss that smirk off his face. Instead, she folded her arms over her middle and looked out the window. "Well, me either."

Jason looked at her for a long moment as he pulled up to the gate. "I have something to say that will 100 percent annoy you."

Mallory rolled her eyes. "What is it?"

"It's a bit of a cliché, but in your case, it definitely applies."

"Go ahead, Jason—we don't have all day. We have locations that *must be nailed down*, remember?" she asked, mimicking his stern instructions earlier.

"Okay, here goes—you're adorable when you're mad."

She stared at him. What nonsense was this? "Are you kidding me? No I'm not."

"Yeah, you are," he said, and grinned. "I told you you'd be annoyed."

"You know how I hate that sort of thing." She'd once had to sit him down and explain to him how some of his remarks could be viewed as sexist.

"Oh, I know."

"You're just saying it to get my goat."

"I don't want your goat, I'm saying it because it is true. I could kiss you right now."

She couldn't keep the grin from her face. "Well, don't. You're driving."

They drove into King Harbor and down a leafy street to what looked like a grand mansion. "What is this?"

"The Bickmore," Jason said. "It used to belong to a film star. It's been converted to a luxury hotel."

It looked extremely luxurious. Mallory was beginning to think she could get used to this life of private planes, summer estates, and luxury hotels.

"I'll be right back." Jason hopped out, grabbed her things from the back hatch and jogged up the steps to the entrance. Not five minutes later, he was in the car again.

"That was quick," Mallory said as he strapped into his seat.

"Yep. The Blackthornes keep a couple of rooms there in the summer for an overflow of guests." He looked at her. "You're getting one of them for as long as I need you."

"I'm getting one for as long as I agree to stay."

"Same thing," he said. He reached behind her and pulled out a notebook and handed it to her. "We've got to give a quarry a look. The details are in there."

She opened the notebook and looked at the location. She picked up her phone and googled the quarry in King Harbor, then mapped it. It was about four miles out of town. "Take ninety-five."

"Nah," Jason said, and turned left. "I'll take the one."

"Google says the quickest way is the ninety-five."

"Google isn't always right. I know another way."

"Oh, for the love of—why are men so damn stubborn?" she demanded of the universe.

"Why are women so averse to adventure?" he countered.

"*I'm* not averse to adventure. But I don't like surprises. I had way too many growing up."

"But here's what you're missing—surprises can be good, too. Sit back and relax, darling, and I'll take you on one."

"Yes, Mr. Blackthorne. Whatever you say, Mr. Blackthorne."

He put his hand on her knee and squeezed. "Don't ruin this for me, Mallory. One of my favorite things is scouting locations."

"Then you should scout better ones."

He chuckled. "Meaning?"

"I mean that some of the locations in season one were so uninspired that I cringe when I see them."

"What are you talking about?"

"I've been studying the first season," she said. She reached into her backpack and pulled out her notebook. "And I see places where we could really turn it up a notch if we are going to contend—eyes on the road!" she said as he swerved slightly across the middle lane.

"Like what?" he insisted. "We shot most of the series in the studio last season."

"Like the pier in the final episode," Mallory said. "I'm going to be brutally honest."

"Please."

"You could have afforded to take that scene where Detective Barnes confronts the killer and film it on a rockier, more remote part of the coast, just like the script calls for. But you cheaped out and went to that pier that was so touristy and not at all suspenseful."

"Hey," Jason said, pointing at her. "That was Cass's decision. It might not have been the best location, but it got the job done."

"It wasn't great, Jason."

He looked like he wanted to agree, but he pressed his lips together and looked forward.

"Did you notice in that scene that there are bunch of tourists in the background watching the production?"

"So?"

"So the viewer's eye is drawn to them and not the action. They keep moving around and pointing at the actors."

He frowned and shook his head. "I saw that scene and I didn't notice the tourists. We cleared the set."

"Really?" She couldn't help a smug smile. "It's pretty hard to clear a big public pier. You should follow some of the live tweets when the episode airs if you don't believe me."

"What?" Now he looked horrified.

"Live tweets. People who watch the show and tweet about it."

"I know what live tweets are. I mean, why are you saying that?"

"Because they will, and they will tweet things that are not the most complimentary things. It's a game to them—they are looking for a "gotcha." Remember during the final episodes of *Game of Thrones* how all the online talk was about the misplaced coffee cups and water bottles?"

Jason nodded.

"My point is, why give viewers an opportunity to take others out of the story with that sort of thing if we don't have to?"

He glanced at her, then looked straight ahead. "Interesting," he said as they pulled into the quarry parking lot.

"What is this place?" Mallory asked.

"And old abandoned quarry. It sits empty now, collecting graffiti and beer bottles. Cass has the idea that we can use this as the place where the killer keeps his victims." They got out of the car and walked to the edge of the quarry. "What do you think?" Jason asked her.

Mallory looked into the hole. It wasn't particularly deep. "I think, are you kidding?"

"The idea is that they can't get out, and what is more terrifying than to be stuck in a giant hole?"

Cass was crazy, that's what Mallory thought. She looked down to where rainwater had collected at the bottom. This looked like a shooting nightmare, and frankly, the quarry itself didn't look like it was inescapable. She looked around for a way into the pit. "What are the alternatives to this?"

"An old warehouse on the other side of King Harbor."

Which was probably perfect, but of course Cass was going to go for either the laziest or most impossible shot. She walked around the edge of the quarry to where a small chasm ran up to the edge of the pit. There was an earthen ledge below. She crouched down, then hopped into it.

"Hey!" Jason shouted. A moment later, his head appeared above her. "You're not exactly dressed for spelunking."

"You know what is wrong with this location? It would require some manipulation to make it look really inescapable. And there is the problem of how the killer would get his victims out. I mean, presumably he's not going to give them a ladder because they would take it and escape. Did you and Cass talk about that?"

Jason crouched down. "Rope."

"And the killer is going to haul them up like sacks of flower." She looked around. "I don't know, Jason. Look at it. There are too many places someone desperate to escape could get a hand-hold." She turned back and hiked up onto a rock that protruded from the side. Jason grabbed her hand and hauled her out, and she landed on a patch of earth right before him.

His gaze was on her mouth, and it had the effect of stirring her blood. "We could cover it with scenery."

They were standing so close, their bodies were almost touching. "We could. But let's go look at the warehouse."

"Already scouted," he said, and his gaze moved lower, to the vee or her blouse.

"Humor me."

He slowly lifted his gaze. "Cass likes the pit, Mallory. He's the director."

"Does that mean you won't even entertain any other ideas?"

He shifted closer. She lifted her chin. She wondered if he would kiss her, or if he would realize they were in the middle of a workday. "Of course I will. But I may not agree with the other ideas I hear."

She smiled. "I just ask that you listen." She stepped away from all that heat and possibility. "Can we go see that warehouse?" She started toward the car.

Jason caught up to her just as she reached the door of the Range Rover and opened it for her. But he didn't move out of the way so she could get in. "I will show you the warehouse," he said. "But on one condition."

"Okay. What is it?"

He touched the back of his hand to her cheek. "You call the head writer on the way and let him know we need to cut the scene where the girl runs through the forest at night in episode eight."

"What? *Why?*" Mallory protested. "That's the best scene of this whole series!"

"Because we've got to cut seven minutes in that episode, and that's the easiest place to cut."

"Let me guess," Mallory said. "Cass? He hates night shoots. He tells everyone who will listen how much he hates night shoots."

Jason tucked her hair behind her ear, then let his hand fall to her shoulder. "You have to trust me on this, Mallory. Cass and I know what we are doing."

She supposed that meant she did not know what she was doing. She supposed that meant that while he would tolerate her suggestions, he wasn't open to taking them. And there it was again—the overwhelming urge she always had in his presence—to punch him in the mouth and then kiss him silly.

But Mallory climbed into the vehicle and pulled out her phone to call the head writer.

CHAPTER ELEVEN

THE WAREHOUSE SMELLED WORSE THAN THE FIRST TIME Jason had stepped foot into it with Cass. It was freezing inside, and something was dripping from the ceiling. He noticed dark stains on the floor that he and Cass had decided was rust, but neither of them wanted to examine too closely to be sure.

"Gross," Mallory said.

"Told you," Jason said, poking her in the side.

"But it's perfect. How can you and Cass not think this is perfect?"

Jason looked at her sidelong. "Just curious—do you think this is perfect because Cass doesn't think it's perfect?"

"My opinion has nothing to do with Cass," she said primly. Then shrugged. "Not 100 percent, anyway. Hey, look at this!" she said, and walked into the middle of the space. She held up her hands, forming a frame. "See that shaft of light coming in from the window? It's dark and creepy, and that light gives us just enough to see. So imagine the camera pans over this gross place, and the viewer thinks it is empty, but then you see something, like a foot or a hand, in the narrow shaft of light—and the camera shows us three women huddled together in the corner looking terrified." She dropped her hands. "This place is perfect."

Jason looked at the shaft of light.

Mallory walked back to where he stood and made a frame with her hands again, just in front of him. She slowly moved them around to the corner.

Jason had to admit, it was pretty good. It was creepy. And it wasn't a big pit, which, he had to agree, would be a filming nightmare. He'd said as much to Cass, and Cass said Jason had no balls. Sometimes he suspected that Cass didn't respect him, that he threw things at him to see how he would handle them. He suspected the pit was one of those things.

Mallory dropped her hands and turned to look at him with a hopeful expression. "So you know the scene when the killer comes in," she said, and began walking through it, talking through every step of the scene, pointing out the camera angles. Jason was impressed—she'd definitely done her homework. She had a clear vision. As she talked, he thought of all the times she'd suggested things and he'd essentially patted her on the head and sent her on her way because he was too busy to hear them. Jason could really be a moron sometimes.

She was looking at him with so much hope and eagerness that he couldn't look away from her. He knew how that felt. How important it was to find someone who heard your ideas and liked them. But he also had Cass to consider, a world-class director with a short temper, legally contracted to him to direct these episodes. The location really was his call.

"Well?" Mallory asked.

"I will ask Cass to reconsider," he offered. "That's all I can do."

"*Yes!*" Mallory cried, and pumped both fists into the air.

Jason had a strong urge to kiss her right now. But he didn't want her to think he was offering to speak to Cass because he was attracted to her. "It's his call, Mallory. I can't make any promises."

"I know, I know, and I would never expect you to," she interjected eagerly. "Just that you're willing to ask him, it means...well, it means a lot, Jason." She beamed a smile at him.

Damn, but that smile could inspire a guy to do all kinds of things that were probably not advised. He wanted to make her happy, he did, but he knew without asking that Cass would say no. Cass never bowed to the opinions of others. He was very much a my-way-or-the-highway sort of man. He wanted to tell her that Cass probably wouldn't consider it, but she looked so excited he couldn't do it. So he held out his hand to her. "Let's go. There is a cove I want to check out."

Mallory was still grinning as she slipped her hand into his.

The cove Jason had in mind was a good thirty minutes outside of King Harbor on a strip of coastline that was too rocky and steep in places for most tourists and beach walkers. As they drove along the coast, Mallory chatted how she would direct that scene in the warehouse if it were her. How she thought she could wring more emotion out of the actors than the script portrayed. Listening to her, Jason was a somewhat astounded that she knew so much about the details of the shoot. When he looked at her, he saw an assistant. Someone to find his phone and get his coffee. He hadn't considered her own ambitions, and how she had thought so much about how the show was being guided and shot.

They reached a small inlet on the edge of a promontory. Just around that point was the cove. At the entrance to the inlet was a weathered wooden cabin painted blue. The words *Dead Man's Cove* was painted in faded white letters over the door. On the outside walls hung a line of boat fenders, fishing nets and lobster pots, and a plastic shark.

"This looks ocean-y," Mallory said. "What are we doing here?"

"I'm going to hire a boat," Jason said. "Then we're going around that promontory," he said, pointing, "and take a look at Dead Man's Cove."

"Great," she said, sounding less than enthused.

They walked up to the porch of the building. A sign proclaimed the sea shop was open from ten until four. When Jason opened the door a little bell tingled overhead. He and Mallory stepped inside the crowded room and waited for someone to appear. A few minutes later, a man who looked to be in his fifties with a scraggly gray beard, wearing a thick, cable-knit sweater, stepped up behind the counter.

"How can I help you folks?"

"We'd like to hire a boat to go and have a look at the cove," Jason said, and glanced at Mallory. "They say bootleggers used to run out of the cove."

"Or into the cove, depending on what you hear," the man said.

"I'm sorry?" Jason asked.

"Just saying," the man said. "My grandpa always said old man Blackthorne didn't take kindly to bootleggers hustling his part of the ocean. Shot and killed a man off one boat who was trying to get to the cove."

Jason snorted at that absurdity. "Old man Blackthorne had his own operation."

"Sure he did. Bigger and faster boats, too. He told his men to shoot first and ask questions later."

Jason shook his head at what he hoped was an absurd rumor. "I never heard this story, and I'm a Blackthorne."

That declaration did not faze the old man. He handed Jason a ledger to sign, waiving any liability. "Course you didn't hear it. You know better than me how the Blackthornes keep their secrets."

Something clicked in Jason's chest. He knew that very well—nothing should ever besmirch the Blackthorne name. "When was this, exactly?" he asked curiously.

"Prohibition, a'course," the man said. He stood up and took a key from one of several hanging from a pegboard. "Blue boat, slot two. If you see any skeletons in the cove, you'll know why." He chuckled at his joke, revealing a few missing teeth.

"Thanks," Jason said, and picked up the key.

"That was strange," Mallory said as she and Jason stepped outside. "Do you think that could be true?"

"I honestly don't know," Jason said. He was thinking about the night Aunt Claire disappeared. She'd said to Uncle Graham she'd kept his secret, and he and his cousins had tried to guess what the secret could be. Could *this* have been the secret? That their great-grandfather had killed a man?

"What's the matter?" Mallory asked.

Jason shook his head. "It's a long story. My aunt and uncle are having…well, marital problems, I guess. They split up recently and when she left, she told him she'd kept his secret, or something to that affect. My cousins and brothers and I have been trying to figure out what that meant. I'm just wondering if it was a murderous relative." He smiled at her. "Trust me, Blackthorne Enterprises wouldn't want that floating around."

The blue boat they'd rented was hardly bigger than a tub, with a small outboard motor attached to it.

Mallory immediately asked for a life vest.

Jason handed her one. "It's just around the bend up here," he said, pointing.

"Are you really going to try and ferry actors and crew and equipment in these boats?" she asked as she strapped tightly into the life vest.

"We'd obviously use bigger boats," he said. "My cousin Devlin can hook us up." She looked very wary as she inspected the boat, and alarmingly cute in her blue pantsuit and life vest. The prosecutor, out for a swim.

Jason helped her into the boat and tried hard not to laugh at the way she held her arms out in an attempt to provide ballast. "It's not funny!" she shouted at him.

He was still grinning as he jumped in after her and pushed the boat away from the dock, then throttled slowly away from the shore. While Mallory gripped the sides of the boat, he opened up the motor and cleared the buoys, then moved around the promontory.

When he was a teen, Dead Man's Cove was the destination of the more adventurous kids. He hadn't been out here in years, and the cove was much smaller than what he remembered, nothing but a strip of white sand beach and rocky walls that formed a small cliff. Fitting a film crew in here would be tight. He had not brought Cass here yet—Cass was determined to film the boat scenes in King Harbor. But Jason had wanted to see this again. He motored the boat in as close as he could get, then leapt out and dragged it onto the sand.

Mallory was still gripping the sides of the boat. "This isn't going to work."

"You haven't even seen the cave. Come on, Mal—give it a chance."

She pressed her lips together. She gave him a curt nod, kicked off her impractical shoes—"I just got these," she said, miffed about them—and rolled up her pant legs. She inched toward the front of the boat and refused to let go of it with one hand as she reached for Jason with the other.

"Have you never been on a boat before?"

"No! We were not boat people. *Help* me," she begged.

He was laughing when he reached into the boat, put his hands on her waist, and lifted her out. She slid down his body until her feet touched the sand. He smiled.

She glared at him. "What are you doing?"

"Helping. Like you asked."

One corner of her mouth quirked up and she gave him a push away from her. "Stop smiling at me like that. And stop making me do things like ride in little wooden tubs out into the ocean."

"For the record, it is a bona fide boat, and I can't stop smiling at you like that. You are adorable, and I keep thinking about last night."

She sort of laughed and gasped at the same time. "You can't say I'm adorable and you can't think about last night, Jason! We're technically at work, so it's super inappropriate. Don't you know anything?"

"You can't tell me you never think of super inappropriate things at work. Because we both know you do."

"You don't know that," she said, laughing it off, and began to carefully pick her way through the sand toward the cave.

Jason followed her, and when they reached the cave, he went in first, climbing up onto a rock and then helping Mallory up. This, too, was smaller and less sinister than he remembered. It was really hardly a cave it all, very shallow in breadth and in depth. It was hard to believe anyone had ever run any sort of operation out of here.

"Could the killer reasonably stash his boat here or in the cove?" Mallory asked, peering around him to see into the cave. "It doesn't need to be a secret place. Just some place no one would suspect. Any marina would do."

"If this place was good enough for bootleggers, I'd say it's good enough for our guy."

Mallory didn't seem convinced. She tried to lean around him to look again, but when she did, her foot slipped and she almost tumbled into the water. Jason caught her before that could happen, and when he did, he felt something catch in his back.

He pulled her into his arms, twisting her around so that her back was to the wall of the cave.

"Oh my God!" she said breathlessly. "I almost fell in!"

"I've got you," Jason said. She was clinging to his arms, her eyes wide with the fright that near fall had given her. "Mallory…do you know how to swim?"

"No! Do you see how dangerous this is? We can't film in here!"

"If we had another boat for the camera and some scaffolding for the lights," he said, looking up, "we'd be fine. This water isn't very deep. Maybe up to your waist at low tide."

Her eyes widened. "It would take our entire budget to set this up. What is *wrong* with you and Cass? Do you have any idea how much these things—"

Jason silenced her with a kiss. Yes, he knew how much these things cost. Yes, he could see it was impractical. He would argue with her in a minute, but she looked so lush that he couldn't help himself, and neither could Mallory, because the moment he put his lips to hers, she softened, sinking into him, like she'd been waiting for that kiss all day.

He nibbled at her bottom lip, then slipped his tongue into her mouth. Mallory's hands went up around his neck, her fingers sliding into his hair. Jason shifted her backward, so that she was leaning against the rock wall.

"*Now* what are you doing?" she murmured against his mouth.

"Kissing you, obviously. And just so we're clear, you're kissing me back, right?"

"I am. But it's still inappropriate."

He didn't care. He moved to her neck.

"We shouldn't do this," she said through a soft moan. "This is hardly the place for a grand make-out session. We are barely able to stand on this rock as it is."

"We are standing just fine. Where's your sense of adventure?" he asked, and slipped his hand into the waistband of her pants.

Mallory gasped with surprise; her eyes fluttered open and she looked at him as he undid the button of her pants with his thumb. "You are the *devil*," she whispered.

"Thank you," he whispered back, and slid his hand deeper into her pants.

Mallory's gaze did not move from his, challenging him. "This is insane," she insisted, and slid her hand to the front of his shorts, feeling his hardness.

"And exciting. Admit it." He began to stroke her through the thin fabric of her panties. "Looks like forbidden fruit turns us both on, doesn't it?" It was a rhetorical question—it definitely turned her on. She was damp, already slick with just a bit of kissing. "*Doesn't it?*" he insisted.

"A little," she murmured, and closed her eyes.

Jason smiled into her hair and rubbed her, slipping his

fingers under the fabric of her panties. "You know what else turns me on?" he asked, and lightly bit her neck.

"What?" she managed.

"Making you come," he muttered, and with two fingers, quickened the pace. She began to move against his hand, and it seemed to Jason that the water was lapping the rock in time with their rhythm. He stroked her until she made a soft cry and dropped her forehead to his shoulder, shuddering with her release.

He kissed her neck, her ear, her cheek. That had been hugely arousing.

She took gulps of air until her breathing had returned to normal and he'd removed his hand. She sighed and stared up at him with eyes glassy with contentment. "Happy now?"

Jason grinned. "Exceedingly." He kissed her mouth. "Lets get out of here. We still have one more place to see."

Mallory buttoned her pants. "This is so crazy, Jason. What are we doing?"

She didn't mean the question to be answered, he took it, but he was wondering the same thing. His thoughts were confused. Between Darien, and the crazy tension between him and Mallory, and the problems with Cass, and the crisis of having to move this series ahead without a star, he wondered why he chose now to start this with Mallory. It was a question that needed answering, and was going to answer her. When the time was right.

"We're definitely crossing this cove off the list, right?" she asked. She clung to his arm as she stepped off the rock and made a little leap onto the sand just beyond.

"Probably."

"Definitely," she countered. "It's too expensive."

"Then where do you suggest the killer hide his boat?"

"What about the pier? It's not exactly on the beaten path."

They continued their discussion of the killer's need to move relatively unseen as Mallory strapped into her life vest and carefully climbed back on the boat.

In the car, Mallory had a message on her phone from the head writer. She put her on speaker and the three of them talked about alternatives to cutting the forest scene and still shaving seven minutes.

They carried on as if nothing had happened last night or in the cove. They carried on like they always did, as if the crazy tension between them didn't exist, except when it was unbearable, and Jason guessed they would carry on like that until it erupted again.

It was a full day by the time they were done. Jason dropped Mallory at the Bickmore and drove out to the estate to get his things. He stopped by Nana's cottage to tell her he'd be working in town for a few days.

He found his grandmother on her porch in a rocking chair enjoying her standard cocktail—whisky, straight up.

"Hey, Nana," he said, and leaned down to kiss her cheek.

"There you are. I wondered if you'd gone back to Los Angeles."

"Not yet," he said. "Mind if I join you?"

"You know where I keep the good stuff," she said, and nodded to the door of her cottage.

Jason went inside to her kitchen and poured a little of the Blackthorne whisky, then joined his grandmother on the porch. He filled her in on what had been happening with the show and the scandal of Darien as they watched sailboats heading back to the harbor.

When he finished his drink, Jason got up to go. "Got some work to do, Nana. There's still plenty of L.A. hours left in the workday."

"All right," she said.

Jason started for the porch stairs, but he paused and glanced back at his grandmother. "By the way...an old guy over at Dead Man's Cove told me an interesting story today."

"What's that?"

"He said that Great-grandpop killed a bootlegger for working out of his part of the ocean."

Nana stared at him. "Alistair?"

Jason nodded. "I told him I'd never heard that, and he said Blackthornes liked to keep their secrets. And, you know, Aunt Claire said she'd been keeping Uncle Graham's secret. Was that it, Nana? That sounds like something Uncle Graham would not want floating around out there. Do you think—"

"No, I do not," she said flatly. "Whoever told you that is talking about that bootlegger that drowned off Dead Man's Cove. He wasn't murdered! He and his band of nitwits drank the whisky they were bootlegging, and he got so drunk he fell off and drowned. His body washed up in that cove and your great-grandfather sent a crew down there to haul his dead ass out of there. That was just rumor going around because the man's kin wouldn't accept that he was stupid enough to drown himself."

Jason chuckled. "Good to know. The story was just crazy enough that I couldn't help wonder."

"Don't wonder anymore," Nana said, and smiled. "Help me out of this chair before you go."

Jason got her up, kissed her goodbye, and told her he'd come out again in a few days. He watched her go into her house, then headed for the Bickmore.

He texted Mallory when he arrived to let her know he was there.

She texted back:

You have to come to my room. Second episode tonight.

Jason joined her. They ordered room service and watched the second episode of *Bad Intentions*.

As they watched, Mallory pointed out some things that she thought could have been better. And as much as Jason hated to admit it—he respected Cass, thought he was an excellent director—he had to agree with Mallory.

This wasn't the first time he was hearing these thoughts, and not just from Mallory. Crew members had made off-the-cuff remarks about a scene, and certainly Neil Tarelli was not a fan of Cass's direction. But Jason hadn't seen this episode since they'd finished it, and now, with the benefit of time, he could see what Mallory and others were talking about. There *were* clunky transitions. There were places the lighting was horrible, which, he supposed, they knew, as they'd fired the gaffer. But this seemed more than just a bad gaffer. This seemed like laziness.

There was one scene where the character of the detective found out his sister had died. This was a central motivating factor to the detective's motivation. But the news was so glossed over that Jason realized by the time the first season ended, he'd forgotten about the sister.

When the episode ended, and Mallory was chattering about production schedules, Jason couldn't stop thinking about how Cass had framed the episode. He thought back to when he and Cass had inked the deal with him. Cass had been enthusiastic, full of ideas. But by the time they started filming, he'd begun to complain. Nothing had changed between pre-production and production with the series. Everything was as Jason had envisioned and Cass had wholeheartedly endorsed.

Something felt weird and off, like a thread had been pulled when he'd fired Darien, and now things were slowly unraveling.

CHAPTER TWELVE

JASON EXCUSED HIMSELF WITH THE EXCUSE OF BEING
exhausted—Mallory was, too—and with a lingering kiss, he
left her room.

When Mallory closed the door behind Jason that night,
she stood there a minute, chewing on her bottom lip. Had she
pushed too hard during the airing of episode two? She'd had
her notes ready. She'd pointed out various things as they'd
watched. She'd been very careful to mention the masterful
things she saw in Cass's direction—he really was amazing at
directing a lot of action sequences. But that was the thing
with Cass—he was a master when he wanted to be. And
when he didn't want to be a master, he rushed through scenes
and left them, in her studied opinion, unfinished.

Mallory's desire was for *Bad Intentions* to be the best
crime drama on anyone's screen. But she understood why no
one wanted to listen to her. Who the hell was she, the
showrunner's assistant, to offer her opinion on Cass Farenthold? She got that, she really did…but it didn't mean her
ideas or opinions were wrong. It didn't mean she was
clueless.

Mallory was not going to stop trying to improve this show. She was never going to accomplish her goals if she wasn't bold enough to speak up and make her thoughts known. *Nevertheless, she persisted.*

But maybe her delivery could use some work. Maybe she shouldn't have asked Jason why Cass had signed on to do *Bad Intentions*.

"I'd like to think he believed in the project."

Yeesh. Of course he would. She'd shrugged and said, "I just wondered. There are all these rumors about him pursuing a development deal with Sony." She'd only heard bits and pieces through the gossip grapevine on set, which was a healthy, living thing that had sunk its tentacles in everyone. There might not be any truth to it at all, but it made sense to her that Cass had signed on with Jason, and then a better deal came along, and he was contractually obligated to continue with Jason until his two-year term was up, or the series was cancelled. It would explain a lot, wouldn't it? It was entirely possible she was too cynical, but she knew what it looked like when someone wanted out of a job. Her father made Cass look like a baby in that regard.

"Everyone in this business is always angling for a bigger, better deal," Jason had said evenly. "But that doesn't mean he wasn't interested in this one."

He hadn't seemed surprised by the rumor. He'd seemed annoyed by it.

She went back to the desk in her room and opened her laptop with the intent of emailing her sister, but was surprised to find an email from Morning Moonlight Films in her inbox.

Hi Mallory, Kelly here! We were wondering if you'd given any more thought to joining our team! Just a reminder that we believe we have a competitive compensation package and opportunities to work on some really great projects!

Kelly recapped the points she'd gone over with Mallory in her interview.

It was a good opportunity for her. Mallory could accept the job now. Just hit send. If she accepted the job, she'd be working with small projects almost immediately, such as corporate videos and commercials. Admittedly, it was not exactly the content she wanted for herself, but that didn't matter. This was a start. It was experience. And that was exactly what she needed. She didn't want to be an assistant, she wanted to be part of the creation of the content and the final product.

Her fingers hovered over the keys…but she didn't accept. She thanked Kelly for her email and asked for one more week to consider the offer.

Kelly must have been sitting at her computer, because she quickly replied.

Please take more time if you need it. But we'll need an answer pretty soon, particularly if we need to make other arrangements.

Mallory assured her she understood and would have her answer in a week.

She closed her laptop and leaned back in her chair, gazing out the window at the lights in the harbor. She had lost her fool mind, hadn't she? This was the opportunity she'd been chasing for ten years. Why hadn't she jumped on it? Why was Jason's face dancing in front of her mind's eye? Was she really going to lose this opportunity because she had the hots for the boss? It was so unlike her, so irresponsible. If Inez were here, she might have slapped some sense into her.

Call it a gut feeling, but Mallory was not ready to pull the plug on Blackthorne Entertainment. She didn't know what was happening with her and Jason, other than this crazy and wild sexual thing. What had happened in the cave today was beyond exciting. But where the last twenty-four hours had left her and Jason, she hadn't had time or courage to face. It didn't take a genius to recognize that this was not a sustainable boss-subordinate relationship. To put it more bluntly, which Inez would certainly do if she was here, this was a disastrous relationship, one that had big neon warning signs stacked all around it. This was the kind of thing that could easily break her heart.

What she needed was for Inez to talk some sense into her. She picked up her phone.

"Hey!" Inez said when she answered. "How's life in Maine with your crazy-ass boss?"

Mallory smiled into the phone. "He's super rich, that's what."

"And that's a surprise?"

"No, I mean he's *super* rich, like Mr. Darcy and Pemberley rich."

Through the phone, she could hear Inez's soft intake of breath. "Dude. Tell me everything."

"You would not believe the summerhouse, Inez. I thought it was a resort! It sits right on the ocean. Oh, and he flew me out in a private plane."

"*What?* What about the environment you're always going on about?"

"Someone was going to be riding in that plane regardless of the damage to the ozone layer, and it might as well have been me."

Inez laughed. "Okay, so what's going on with Darien Simmons? The news is full of his face. Did he really force her into a bathroom?"

Mallory gasped. "What? I hadn't heard that."

"You hadn't *heard* that? The girl went to *People* and told them he pushed her into a bathroom and locked the door behind him and started taking her clothes off. Such a sick fuck, am I right? Jason must be spinning. How is it with him, anyway, other than he's super rich? Is he driving you crazy?"

Not in the way Inez meant. "No, he's been...he's been good," Mallory said, a little too brightly. "I mean, things are insane right now, obviously."

There was a slight pause on the other end. "What are you not telling me?" Inez instantly insisted. "What dick move has he done?"

"Nothing!"

There was a long pause on Inez's end. "Jesus Mallory, you're not doing his *laundry* are you?"

"No!" she said firmly. At least she hadn't yet. "Of course not, Inez," she said firmly. Ah, the insistence of innocence by the guilty. "He has people to do that," she said, thinking of Pam. "But we've, ah...we've sort of scratched the itch, if you know what I'm saying."

"Oh my God!" Inez shrieked. "Mallory! What the hell are you doing? You *love* your job, remember?"

"I know," Mallory groaned.

"There is no way this is going to work! Are you insane? What do you think he's going to do the moment a hot actress joins the cast?"

"What?"

"I'm *saying*, he's going to fuck you and then he's going to dump you when the bigger better thing comes along."

She didn't have to be crude, but then again, Mallory could count on Inez to give it to her straight. "He's not like that, Inez." She knew, the moment the words left her mouth, how ridiculous she sounded.

"Like hell he isn't. Every straight man in Hollywood is like that. Girl, you need to take that other job. Don't let your vagina do your thinking for you, Mallory."

"I know, I know," Mallory said. This was exactly what she'd called Inez for, but she wasn't liking the straight talk. What she *really* wanted was for Inez to tell her it was fabulous, and he was wonderful. She wanted this thing with Jason to turn into something more. And she didn't want to leave him in the middle of all this chaos. "I know what you are saying is true. And I should take the other job. But I can't leave him in a lurch, Inez. I can't."

"Mallory. It is not your lurch. Seriously, you have to protect yourself. These things never work out. Look at Darien Simmons—"

"Inez! Jason didn't *assault* me! It's a very mutual thing."

"I know, I get it, but I'm saying that he's still a man in Hollywood, and he will sleep with you and he will use you to get through this crisis, and then where will you be? You will have passed up the other job. If you want to sleep with him, take the other job and sleep with him! But don't do it while you're working for him."

"That other job is a pay cut, remember? And we already can hardly afford the rent as it is."

"Now you're making excuses. You take that other job, and you'll get it back tenfold when your career takes off. No gain without risk, baby."

They talked a little more about what was going on with Inez, and Inez issued her warning again before she hung up. "You are headed for a fall," she said.

Inez was right in everything that she said. And still, Mallory hesitated. Her crush, or her attachment, or whatever it was she had for Jason Blackthorne was strong. What *did* she have for Jason Blackthorne? Was it love? Surely it wasn't *love*. Or was it? Sure, she admired him. He was funny and he could be so kind—she knew he was the one who had paid the receptionist's car repair bill without her knowing it. Tamra was still talking about her secret angel. But Jason also drove her nuts with his disorganization and his lack of consideration at times. And yet…she had never been so drawn to a guy as she was to him.

She was mulling it over when her phone buzzed. She glanced at the screen and picked up the call. "Hey, Megs," she said to her sister. "What have Mom and Dad done now?"

In the ensuing conversation about Dad's new get-rich quick scheme—flipping houses, for God's sake—Mallory forgot about Jason and her job offer for the night.

CHAPTER THIRTEEN

IN THE BICKMORE LOBBY, JASON WAS SITTING ON ONE OF THE antique settees. He was on his phone, wrapping up the reservation of the warehouse for filming—Cass would not be happy, but he'd made an executive decision—when he noticed a pair of legs walking down the staircase and glanced up. He was slightly startled to realize those were Mallory's killer legs coming down the stairs. She was wearing a navy dress with little white and blue flowers, and a skirt that brushed her knees. And a pair of red heels that he imagined her wearing with nothing else.

"Thanks, Ben," he said to the man who owned the warehouse. He was an old family friend. "My lawyer will be in touch. I really appreciate it." He clicked off and slowly stood. His back was still bothering him where he'd tweaked it yesterday.

"Wow," he said as she walked to where he stood. "You look *great*, Mallory." He deliberately allowed his gaze to move appreciatively down the length of her.

"Thanks!" She looked down. "Inez got to keep this dress

after her stint on *CSI Miami*." She lifted her gaze to his. Her eyes were shining. She was happy to see him.

"Are you ready?" he asked.

She rolled her eyes. "Am I ever *not* ready?"

"Rhetorical question," he said with a grin. "That's what makes you such a great assistant."

Mallory smiled back, too, but it was a little thin. As if she found the word distasteful. He packed that away for the time being.

On the way to Boston, she filled him in on the latest gossip and press coverage of Darien Simmons. "The *Hollywood Reporter* is saying that another woman has come forward," she said, reading off her phone.

"Great," Jason snapped. His hand fisted against the steering wheel. "I never heard anything like this about him. Did you?"

"No, but I'm not exactly plugged in. Oh, great—here is the official statement from the lawyer."

She read it out loud to him, and Jason dictated a couple of changes, making it a stronger denial of any knowledge and an even stronger statement of intolerance for that sort of behavior. Next, they went over the production schedule Mallory had apparently reworked this morning. Jason silently marveled at how efficient she could be. He would kill for a tenth of that efficiency.

They chatted about how quickly they needed one of the actors on board, assuming the auditions went well.

They had just entered downtown Boston when Jason asked if there was anything else they needed to talk about. His mind was already a million miles ahead—past the auditions and on to the shooting that would start in days.

"Actually," Mallory said, and folded her hands neatly over her lap. "There is one thing."

"Yeah? What's that?" Jason asked as he glanced at his watch.

"I've been offered a job at a small film company."

He jerked his gaze to her and in doing so, very nearly jerked the car into a parked truck. "What are you talking about?"

"It's a small independent film company. Morning Moonlight Films?"

He'd never heard of them. He shook his head. "Doing what? CEO's assistant? How much are they offering you? I'll give you a raise if that's it."

She pressed her lips together a moment, as if she were collecting herself. "It's not an assistant position, Jason. It's an offer to join their stable of directors."

"*Director?*" He couldn't keep the surprise from his voice. She had no experience in directing. None. She was an assistant to a showrunner. Yeah, okay, she said she'd made some short films, but high school kids across America were making short films. That did not make her a hireable director.

"I have done some short films," she said defensively, as if reading his mind. "They saw my work in a couple of contests, and they asked me to interview, and I did, and now, they want to add me to their roster."

"Like, for pay?"

"Of course for pay!" she said, miffed. "It's a *job*, Jason."

"Okay, okay," he said, more to himself than to her, because his heart was suddenly racing. "Directing what, exactly?"

"Corporate films. Commercials."

"Okay," he said carefully.

"It's experience, Jason. And I need experience if I'm ever going to get a leg up. I want to pursue my dreams, and I can't do that being an assistant for the rest of my life."

"I know," he said. His thoughts were firing like pistons. She wouldn't really take that job, surely. Mallory wanted to tell stories—she didn't want to direct corporate films. Didn't she say she was working on something now? "When did this happen?"

"A few weeks ago."

A few weeks ago, she'd crawled onto his lap in his office. He wondered if by-the-book Mallory had decided then to look for another job. He kept his gaze on the road. "I didn't know you were looking for another job. You never said."

"Well…I think people generally caution against telling their boss they're looking."

Boss. Was that what he was to her? He tended to think of them more as partners. "Makes sense," he said. His grip of the wheel tightened as he tried to imagine doing this work without Mallory to organize him. "So, just curious here—did you do this after I made fun of the motivational posters you hung in the office?"

"What? No!" She gave him that shake of the head women make when they are annoyed.

"Then did you do it after the night in my office?" he asked, and turned his head to look at her.

The color had risen in her cheeks. She folded her arms across her middle. "I don't remember the exact date," she said to the window.

"Well that's interesting, seeing as how exact dates are your thing. Anyway, thanks for letting me know," he said casually.

She eyed him suspiciously. "That's it?"

No, that wasn't it. That wasn't it at all. But Jason didn't know what *it* was yet. He shrugged. "Have you accepted?"

"Not yet."

Well there was a glimmer of hope. "Are you going to accept?"

"I don't know." She glanced down. "I'm thinking about it."

He gripped the wheel even harder.

Neither of them spoke again until they turned into the garage at Hancock Tower.

Jason would have to worry about Mallory later. That was the story of his life—he had to put off worrying about things that mattered to him because there was always a more pressing issue that had to be dealt with. Right now, he needed his game face. He had to get someone on board to take Darien's place before anything else could happen. Full stop.

"Today's goal is keep Cass from trying to bring any other actors in to read for the part, got it?" he said as they walked to the elevators. "We don't have time for that."

"Got it," she said, and the two of them marched through the elevator doors like a pair of soldiers off to their mission. This was just another thing he loved about Mallory—she put her helmet on just like him and threw herself into whatever the task was at hand.

Loved? That word, so casually tossed around his head, edged its way into the forefront of his mind with a big question mark. Was it really so casual? Or was there something to that word?

Really? You're going to do this now?

They rode up to the fifty-third floor, Mallory scrolling through Twitter on her phone, searching for fall out from Darien. The elevator doors opened into a small lobby. A half-moon of a reception desk was centered on a wall emblazoned with enormous letters that spelled out *Blackthorne Enterprises*.

The receptionist, a tall young man who tended to wear

suits so tight that Jason often wondered if he needed implements to button his jacket, stood up as they entered. "Nice to see you again, Jason."

"You too, Chase. How are you?"

"I'm great, thank you," he said. "The conference room is ready for you. Brock would like a word before you get started."

"Okay. Is anyone else here?"

"Not yet. Trey and Graham have a meeting across town this afternoon."

"Hey!" Jason's younger brother Brock walked out into the reception area. Everyone said that Jason and Brock looked the most alike of all of them. Jason would love to believe he was half as put together as his kid brother, but he doubted it.

"Brock, I'd like you to meet Mallory, my assistant."

Brock turned to Mallory and smiled. His appeal ratcheted up when he smiled—it was one of his best assets. Jason had seen it work time and again—girls melted when Brock smiled, and Mallory was no exception. She returned his smiled with a thousand watt one of her own. "Great to meet you," she said, extending her hand. "I've heard a lot about you."

"Oh," Brock said with a playful wince. "I just bet you have. It didn't have anything to do with a logo, did it?"

Jason laughed. They'd gone round and round about that damn logo. "Chase, would you mind showing Mallory to the conference room?" he asked, and to Mallory, "I'll just be a minute."

"This way," Chase said.

When they'd gone round the corner, Jason asked, "What's up?"

Brock's smile was gone. "Come on," he said, gesturing

with his chin in the direction of his office. "He's not in today, but my advice is to avoid Uncle Graham if you can."

"Why?"

Brock glanced over his shoulder. "Some guy from *Vulture* called here, nosing around. He said four women have now come forward to accuse your star of inappropriate behavior, and one of them has even said rape."

Jason's stomach dropped as he followed Brock into his office. He had a flashback to an evening out with Darien and Cass one night. Darien had gotten pretty handsy with the waitress. Jason had told him to cut it out, but the woman had laughed and Darien had smiled, and Jason could feel the vibe between them. That night, Jason and Cass had left but Darien had stayed behind. Had he forced himself on the waitress? Had Jason walked off and left a predator lurking around the woman? She'd seemed totally into it.

"The reporter suggested that Blackthorne Entertainment knew about these allegations—"

"That's bullshit," Jason snapped, but Brock cut him off before he could rant.

"I know, Jason. But you know how Uncle Graham is."

Jason knew how his uncle was, and he couldn't help but wonder if maybe Brock wasn't a little like that, too. He was a bulldog when it came to keeping the Blackthorne name pristine. "I'm handling it, Brock. We have a statement going out today."

"Good," Brock said. "You gotta get in front of it." He looked to the open door, then said softly, "Uncle Graham is making noise about pulling funding from you."

Jason's heart began to pound with the tension he was feeling. "Are you kidding me right now?"

"Don't wig out," Brock said, and patted Jason's chest. "I talked him down. He's just nervous. He thinks there will be lawsuits we could be on the hook for. There's already enough talk going around about him and Aunt Claire, and now, your thing is like a little gas added to his personal fire pit, you know?"

Jason didn't know what the truth was between Uncle Graham and Aunt Claire's separation. But he'd worked too damn hard to be derailed by Uncle Graham's issues.

Voices in the lobby drifted down to Brock's office. "You better go," he said. "By the way, I saw the second episode. It's killer, Jase. You should be proud."

Jason smiled. "Thanks. I am." He walked out of Brock's office and took a shortcut through a break room to the conference room. The very same conference room where he'd stood to beg for the money to get his company off the ground from Trey, Graham and Brock.

Mallory stood up as he entered the room, her phone in her hand. "There is more news about—"

"I heard," he said grimly, just as Chase walked in through a door at the other end of the room. Behind him, Cass swanned into the room wearing a cape and a hat, and a newly trimmed beard. He looked like a portly English butler.

"Hi, Cass," Mallory said cheerfully.

Cass stopped walking. He looked at Mallory, then at Jason, then back to Mallory. "Well, well, well, look who is here. Little Mallory with the big ideas. I suppose you had a hand in our two contestants today."

Mallory's smile instantly faded and Jason was reminded what a jerk Cass could be. "Jason asked me to come to Maine to help him out."

"Oh, I just bet he did," Cass drawled.

"Calm down, Cass," Jason said gruffly. "Why do you have to be rude, man?"

"I'm sorry, am I being rude?" Cass said with feigned

surprise. "I guess because I thought I was quite clear that I needed some time away from this project!"

What was it with artists? Why were so many of them so fucking mercurial? "*Time* is something we don't have. Right now, we've only got a few minutes before the first audition and I want to fill you in on some locations we scouted—"

"*We?*" Cass said sharply. "You scouted locations without me?"

Jason could not believe this guy right now. "What did you think I was going to do? Wait until you'd gone off and smelled some flowers or whatever and put the whole production schedule into jeopardy? We went to the quarry and the warehouse—"

"I specifically ruled out the warehouse!"

"Yeah, well, it's back on the table. We also went to the cove—"

"You can't do this without me," Cass said. "You have no *right* to do this without me. I *must* be involved."

Jason's pulse was beginning to ratchet. Maybe it was the stress of what had happened this week, but he felt like he was one slender moment from punching Cass in the mouth. "I would love for you to be involved," he said as steadily as he could. "But you have to be available. We are on a very strict timetable here, Cass. I've already got crew here."

Chase stepped inside the room. "Mr. Blackthorne? Your guests are here."

"Perfect. Mallory, would you go set it up and bring the first one back?"

"Sure," she said, and walked out of the room.

When she'd gone, Cass turned a murderous look to Jason. "Are you fucking with me, Jason? Your piece of ass waltzes in from L.A. and you are suddenly second-guessing me?"

"Watch your goddam mouth, Cass," Jason said darkly.

"Mallory is probably the most competent person we have on this project. And you know what? She's right about a lot of things a lot of the time. She was damn sure right about the quarry. It's too expensive and impractical. We're going with the warehouse."

"The hell we are—"

"Hello!" Mallory said very brightly, very loudly. She and the first actor had come into the room. "This is Robert Maroney."

"Hello, Cass," Robert Maroney said. "How the heck are you?"

Cass shifted in his seat. "Fine, Robert. Fine."

Jason knew the guy's face. He was a seasoned actor, but when he read with Mallory, his delivery seemed a bit stilted. It could be directed out of him. "Thank you," Jason said when they were done. "We'll be in touch."

"Great," Robert said. "See you guys back in L.A."

Mallory showed him out.

When they were alone again, Cass gave Jason another murderous look. "Are you trying to push me out? Is that what this is?" he asked, with a flick of his wrist toward the door.

"For the love of Christ—*you*'re the one who took yourself out, Cass. I'm trying to keep the damn thing afloat."

The second actor, Trent Hardwick, was the Keanu Reeves lookalike. Introductions were made and the audition began. As Jason watched him, he had to admit that Mallory was right about him—he had the look of someone who'd been through some hard knocks. But he also had that innate appeal. Women would love this guy. *He* loved this guy. When he finished, Mallory smiled at Jason. He could read it in her eyes: *Told you.*

"Thank you," Jason said. "We'll be in touch very soon."

The actor gave them a bit of a salute and walked out of the conference room.

When he was gone, Cass threw his pen down. "I don't want either of them. They are both wooden blocks."

"Really?" Mallory said, surprised. "I thought Trent was really good."

"No one cares what you think, Mallory," Cass snapped. "Haven't you already done enough?"

"Cut it out, Cass," Jason said angrily.

"Darien Simmons was perfect for the role! *Perfect.* He was urbane and sophisticated. These two are great if you're wanting a guide to lead you through the Tetons on a donkey."

"Darien was great in his role," Jason said. "But he's a dick, and he's not here anymore, Cass. I like the second guy, Trent."

Cass looked at the two of them. "*No.*"

"Jesus, Cass. Fine. We'll go with Robert—"

"You're not hearing me, Jason. *Neither* of them. Try again."

Jason pressed his palm to the table and slowly rose, leaned over the table and said slowly, "We are not trying again. We don't have time. Both men were good. And if you won't pick, I will pick for you."

"I suggest you make the time," Cass said coolly. "I will not have my production ruined by actors who can't read their way off a grocery list."

"First of all, it's *my* production. And they are both great actors," Jason said. "What do you think Mallory?"

"Me? Oh, I..." Mallory hesitated. But only a moment. Cass was staring daggers at her and looked like he wanted to come across the table. But Mallory sat a little straighter and said, "I see Trent in this role. I think he's great. Honestly, I think he's a better fit than Darien."

Cass's glare turned murderous. He brought both hands down on the table with a *thwack*. "I am an Oscar nominated director!" he roared.

"So you've mentioned at least a thousand times," Jason said wryly.

"I have directed more films than either one of you have even *seen*. I will *not* take direction from a woman who barely knows her ass from her hand—"

Jason lunged forward, his finger in Cass's face. "You say another word like that and you're off the project," he said furiously. "Stop taking your dissatisfaction out on her."

Cass shoved his finger aside and stood up so quickly his chair toppled backward. He marched toward the door. "Do what you want, Jason. I don't give a fuck." And then he was gone.

Jason and Mallory stood there, stunned. "What just happened?" Mallory asked.

"I think Cass had the mother of all temper tantrums," Jason said, and shoved his fingers through his hair. This was a complete mess. He glanced at Mallory, who was still staring at the door. "Don't take anything he said personally, Mal."

She shook her head. "He's been a prick to me and everyone else for too long. What do we do now?"

"Get Trent's agent on the phone. We need him ready to start shooting in a week." Jason pushed away from the table, and when he did, his back seized. He sucked a sharp breath through his teeth, and grabbed his lower back with his hand.

"Are you okay?" Mallory asked.

"I'm fine," he said, and tried to straighten. "I just tweaked it." At least he hoped that was all he'd done. It felt really painful. "We have to get going," he said, and began to walk, limping a little as he did.

"Jason, you don't look okay. Should we—"

"No. Whatever you're going to say the answer is no. We need to get Neil Tarelli on the phone and get him over to the warehouse. Plus get the lease agreement to the owner of the warehouse." He walked to the end of the conference room, his hand still on his back. "Can you drive?"

"I guess," Mallory said uncertainly, and put her hand to his arm, trying to help hold him up. "Are you sure you're okay?"

"I am," he lied. "It's nothing a couple of aspirin won't knock out." He attempted a smile, but all Jason knew was that he and his back could really go for a stiff drink right now.

CHAPTER FOURTEEN

Jason was not being honest about his back, quite obviously. He could hardly get into the Range Rover and sat crookedly in the passenger seat as Mallory drove back to King Harbor. His face was screwed into a permanent wince as he made his calls.

When they arrived back at the Bickmore, he didn't want to sit in one of the charming antique settees. "Too low," he said. "Tell you what—let's take a break. Meet me down here at six and I'll take you to dinner. There's a little dive down on the pier that makes the best lobster."

"Okay, but shouldn't we—"

"Can we talk later?" he asked quickly. "I'd really like to get an ice pack or something."

"Can I get it for you?" she asked, wincing in sympathy.

"Honestly, Mallory, if you can just get Trent on board, that would be the best thing you could do for me. I've got my back. It's an old baseball injury." He gave her a ghost of a smile and gestured to the stairs.

They walked up together—very slowly, as Jason was having trouble—and when they got to the top, he said, "Six?"

He gave her a ghost of a smile and hobbled down the hall, disappearing around a corner.

Mallory went into her room and sat on the bed. For a moment. She fell on her back and stared up at the plastered medallion ceiling, her thoughts all over the place. One minute, she was thinking of texting him to tell him she had to get back to L.A. The next minute she was wondering if she should call Morning Moonlight and decline.

She rolled over onto her stomach with a moan, found her phone, and called the casting agent to get Trent on board.

At six, she found Jason already in the lobby, dressed in jeans and a T-shirt and sneakers, with a light jacket. He smiled when he saw her, the light filling his hazel eyes. She had a fleeting thought how lovely it would be to see that smile every day of her life. "How are you?"

"Much better. Nothing a few ibuprofen and an ice pack won't fix. It's just a muscle pull. Come on, you're going to love this place."

It turns out that he wasn't kidding about the dive part of that. The place looked so seedy that Mallory was almost afraid to go in. "It's fine," he said, reading her expression, and with his hand firmly on the small of her back, he ushered her inside.

"Hey, Jason! I didn't expect to see you again so soon!" A heavyset woman with a large beehive of hair on top of her head, from which a pencil protruded, grabbed Jason's arm and yanked him forward for a kiss to his cheek. Mallory heard his hiss of pain.

"Hello to you, too, Lorene," he said. "I was telling Mallory here that you can't get better lobster anywhere in Maine."

"Of course not. I know how to pick them. Take a seat and we'll get you hooked up. The works?"

"The works."

She handed them both a bib, and Jason pointed to a table next to four men who looked as if they'd just come in from the water.

They ordered gin and tonics—Jason's idea—and some hush puppies—Mallory's idea—while they waited. Mallory reported the casting agency would have an answer for them tonight. Nick Tarelli had been out to the warehouse and said it was doable. They discussed the cove and whether or not they should try and secure it, but Mallory made some good points about what the costs were going to be trying to move equipment and people in boats.

Their discussion turned to Cass, and in spite of themselves, they were giggling at his performance earlier in the day. "Why might YOU be here?" Mallory said, mimicking his style of delivery.

"It is the quarry or nothing at all!" Jason declared with a dramatic finger jab in the air. He laughed. Then sobered. "I would love to know where he swanned of to."

"Did you call him?" Mallory asked.

Jason shook his head. "I'll get hold of him tomorrow," he said with a flick of his wrist. "He can't have gone far. I have never known someone in this industry who could get their feelings so hurt so fast."

Mallory agreed—Cass was a thin-skinned bully. Weren't they all?

When the lobsters came, and Jason had tutored her in how to get one apart, Mallory finally found the courage to say what she didn't want to say, but had to say. She'd been having too much fun. "I need to go back to L.A. tomorrow."

Jason looked up from his lobster. He had the bib tucked up under his chin, almost like an Elizabethan collar. "So soon?" he asked as he dunked a piece of lobster meat into a small vat of butter.

"I don't have enough clothes. And there is so much that has to be done at the office."

Jason shifted slightly in his seat and grimaced. She wondered if it was his back or the fact that she was leaving. "Why don't you stay two or three days—"

"You promised me, Jason. You said a couple of days. And you know what I am saying is right. We have so much going on. It's not good that we are both out of the office."

He sighed. He leaned back in his chair and drummed his fingers against the table. "You're right," he said reluctantly. "I'll get you a plane in the morning." He was looking at her. Studying her.

"What?"

"You amaze me, Mallory. You know more than I do half the time."

She smiled. "That's my job."

He sat up and leaned forward a little and pushed his plate away, smiling. "I remember the day you came to interview. Do you?"

"Of course I do."

Jason grinned. "You sat on the edge of your seat. You had a binder."

She grinned. "In case you wanted proof of my experience."

His gaze moved down her face, to her bib. "You were wearing this dress with little buttons on the pockets, and one of the buttons was missing."

"No it wasn't."

"Yes it was." He smiled. "Do you want to know what I thought?"

Mallory laughed and yanked her bib free. "I'm not sure. What did you think?"

"You were so business-like. I thought you looked like a librarian. And I thought that was about the sexiest look I'd ever seen on a woman."

Warmth trickled through Mallory. She remembered him, too, perched on the edge of his desk, his gaze steady as he assessed her.

"What did you think?" he asked.

"I thought you were distracted. And that you kept looking at my chest."

"I wasn't looking at your chest. I was looking at that missing button. And I was looking at how pretty you were."

The warmth in her was beginning to turn to heat. "You didn't seem that interested in my experience. You asked some weird question."

"Like?"

"Like, you asked me to look around the office and tell you what I'd do differently."

Jason laughed. "You'd covered every base. I didn't know what to ask. You said you'd need a few days on the job to analyze work flow."

"And you said there was no workflow, there was only chaos, and by the way, did I have "Find my Phone" on my phone and could I show you how it worked."

They were both laughing now. "You said you did, and that did it for me, you were the woman for the job."

They dissolved into laughter. "I really wanted the job," Mallory said through gasps of laughter.

"You were getting the job one way or the other. I was out of options."

"Gee, thanks!" She punched him playfully on the shoulder.

"You were the most attractive woman who had ever applied for a job with me," he said. "That was not the reason I hired, you," he quickly added. "But it didn't hurt anything."

"Really?" She smiled with pleasure.

Jason covered her hand with his. "Let's get out of here."

"Yes. Let's." Mallory felt weak. She could not control her attraction to him—it was out of control, a tornado moving through her and tossing out all common sense.

He paid the bill and they walked out, hand-in-hand. Like they were a couple. Like they could do this for real.

At the hotel, they walked up the stairs together, and at Mallory's door, they paused. She turned around to face him, her back to the door. He braced his hand against the wall, next to her head. "Don't you have some notes or something you'd like to review with me? I mean, if you're flying back to L.A. tomorrow, we should probably review a few things," he said, his gaze sliding past her mouth, to the opening of her shirt.

"You mean episode notes?" she asked as he lazily traced a finger from her throat to the top of her breast. "Suggestions for Cass?"

He looked up. "I wasn't thinking of Cass." He slipped his hand to her nape. "However, I am open up to any suggestion you have."

Mallory opened the door behind her, then grabbed Jason's hand and pulled him inside with her. He had hardly stepped inside before she pushed the jacket from his arms. "I don't know what it is about you, but I kind of want to rip your clothes off every time I see you."

"Same here," he breathed.

She pulled his T-shirt free of his jeans and over his head. Jason wrapped his arms around her and began to walk backward with her to the bed.

"Are we crazy?" Mallory whispered.

"Probably," Jason said, and pressed his lips to the skin of her neck as he worked the buttons of her blouse.

Before he could finish, Mallory twisted him around and pushed him down on the bed. He landed with a grunt of pain. "Sorry!" she cried.

"No I'm okay," he said with a grimace. "I'm really okay." She shimmied out of her pants. "I am so much better now," he said, and propped himself on his elbows to watch her.

She unbuttoned his jeans, and with a little help from him —he could barely lift his hips—she pulled them off of him. "I get to be in charge this time," she said.

"Fantastic," Jason said. "Do to me whatever you want."

With a giggle, Mallory straddled him. She kissed her way down his body, to his cock. She took him in her mouth. Jason groaned, and sank his fingers into her hair. But it was quickly too much. They were both panting, both groaning. "Condom," she said frantically.

"Pants," he said, just as frantically.

She leapt off the bed, dug around his pants, then found his wallet. Tucked inside a pocket was a condom. She crawled back onto the bed and Jason as she ripped the package and slid it on him.

"You are *so* efficient," he muttered.

"Horny," she said against his mouth. She was beyond aroused, too rushed. She should have savored it, but her body was pressing forward, so she slid onto his shaft. Jason anchored her hips with his hands, and they were suddenly a whirl of hands and mouths and movement. They were fucking. There was no other word for it—they were mad for each other, as if each moan spurred the other. She was riding him and he was bucking into her, his hands on breasts. Mallory's release came with a ferociousness that was unlike her, and then Jason's did, too, bucking so hard that they tumbled right off the bed, landing on their sides on the floor. Neither of them had realized how close to the edge of the bed they were.

Mallory burst into laughter. "This has never happened to me before," she said, kissing his face.

"Me either," he agreed. He was grinning. "Could you maybe just…slide off?" he said.

He seemed to be trying to catch his breath. Mallory obliged him and rolled onto her back on the plush carpet. Her heart was still beating hard in her chest. Jason was also on his back, and groped for her hand, holding it tightly in his. "I'm going to miss you."

She laughed. This affection between them was exhilarating. "You'll be back to L.A. soon."

"I know, but this…has been nice. I'm going to miss this."

Mallory wondered if he was referring to the sex or something else. What did he mean? What happened in King Harbor stayed in King Harbor? The thought sobered her, and Mallory slowly sat up, uncertain how she felt about anything. Of course this couldn't continue if they are going to work together. Lord, she could almost hear Inez in her head. She looked at Jason lying beside her. His eyes were closed. "Do you think I should take that job?"

"No," he said emphatically without opening his eyes. "I think you should stay put." He caressed her leg. "What did you think I'd say?"

"I want more, Jason."

"I know you do," he said. "But right now we're in a crisis."

She laughed. "We're always in a crisis."

Jason opened his eyes and turned his head to give her a look.

"I know. Not a joking matter. And not the best time to jump ship."

"I promise we'll talk about it, just as soon as we are shooting. Okay?"

That was another week. "Okay," she said. She didn't want to think about it right now. Mallory stood up and pulled on her pants and shrugged into her shirt, buttoning a few of the buttons. Jason remained on the floor. Mallory looked at him curiously.

"Give me a hand up?" he asked, and winced a little as he lifted his arm.

"Are you okay? Is it your back?"

"I'm just a little stiff."

Mallory helped him to his feet—not without a bit of struggle from him—but when he was on his feet, he took her into his arms. "I'm not going to stay," he said, and moved his hand over her crown.

"Oh." Mallory was surprised by how disappointed she was.

"I have to make some calls," he said apologetically.

He always had to make calls. That was part of the job, obviously. But she wondered, as he ran his hand over her head again, if this is what it would be like. He'd always be off to the next call. *What was she doing?*

Jason kissed the tip of her nose. "Has anyone ever told you how good you are in ye old sack?"

"Stop it," she said, grinning.

"I mean it. You're good at everything, Mallory." He kissed her mouth. A sweet, tender kiss on the mouth. She curled her fingers around the wrist of his hand that cupped her face. This was a different kiss. A very different kiss. It was reverent. Apologetic. "Get some sleep, go back to L.A. tomorrow, and I'll be in touch."

She nodded.

Okay.

Jason found his clothes and stiffly put them on. He walked to the door—it looked like he was leaning to one side. He paused at the door and glanced back, but his head wouldn't turn all the way around. "You wouldn't take that job without talking to me, would you?"

"No. Are you sure you're okay?"

"I'm so good right now," he said with a smile. "And tomorrow my back will be fine," he said with a wink. His gaze lingered on her, but he finally went out.

When the door clicked behind him, Mallory felt sad. She wished she knew how to talk to him about what had happened here in Maine, but God help her, she didn't know how. She didn't know what she wanted to say to even herself.

CHAPTER FIFTEEN

JASON WAS NOT FINE. HE COULD HARDLY MOVE THE NEXT morning. It was like his back had seized up and was crushing the nerves—every movement was excruciating. So he remained flat on his back to make some calls and eat ibuprofen like it was candy. He finally managed to get up, wincing with every step into the shower.

Mallory was gone. He'd asked Ned to pick her up at eight this morning. It was almost noon.

He tried to reach Cass for what he guessed was the tenth time, but there was no answer. Cass was in quite a snit, avoiding Jason's calls. The crew was texting and calling him. They were going to shoot the hospital scenes first, but they needed a director. They needed a call sheet, they needed to know which sequences of which scenes. They needed the director.

Jason couldn't do everything he needed to do with his back killing him. Every movement sent a bolt of lightning down his spine. He needed help.

He was popping more ibuprofen when he got a call from

Marlene, the Blackthorn Entertainment publicist. "What is Cass doing?" she demanded hotly.

"What do you mean?"

"That ass gave an interview to *Good Morning America* and said that Darien's problems were common knowledge."

Jason sat up so fast that he sent his back into spasms. "He did what?" he asked with a hiss of pain.

"You have to fix that," Marlene said. "I can only do so much, but when he's out there running his mouth, it makes it hard. Can you call Cass off?"

"I will try," Jason said darkly.

He tried Cass again, and no surprise, there was no answer. Or the next day. Or the day after that. By then, Jason's back was in such bad shape that he briefly considered throwing in the towel. Just call the whole thing off. *You know that deal you got to produce a series for Netflix? Forget it.* But he didn't.

Marlene called him again. "Who is this Debbie from Blackthorne Enterprises?" she demanded.

And the hits just kept coming. "She is a publicist my family uses from time to time."

"Well, she's been calling making my life harder by insisting we make a distinction between Blackthorne Entertainment and Blackthorne Enterprises. And she wants to know what we're going to do about Cass the Ass."

"I can't get him on the phone," Jason admitted.

When he hung up from Marlene, he had that feeling again, that everything was unraveling. His series. His back. He kept thinking about what Brock had said, how Uncle Graham was thinking of pulling funding because of his fear of lawsuits. If Cass convinced the public that everyone at Blackthorne Entertainment knew about Darien's past and the accusations, he could see that definitely coming to fruition."

"Damn it Cass," he muttered when he tried the director again. "Call me *back*."

On the third day, Jason thought about firing Cass, but had a sneaking suspicion that was exactly what he wanted. He couldn't fathom getting a director at this late date, so he decided to play Cass's game. He instead called in the troops. Meaning, Mallory. "You have to come back."

"No way," Mallory said. "You wouldn't believe the work piling up here."

"Mallory, I need you. I can't do this without you."

She didn't say anything for so long that Jason worried he might have lost the connection. "What's going on?" she asked.

Jason filled her in on Cass's latest antics and the fact he wouldn't call back. "We start shooting in three days and the crew is setting up without any guidance and I don't even have a call sheet. So please, Mallory. This show is so important to me—you have no idea how important."

"I can come," she said slowly. "But with a few conditions."

"Mallory, I—"

"I want to direct."

Jason sighed. "Mallory, you know that I—"

"A few scenes! I'll do the hospital scenes!"

"Cass won't agree," Jason said.

"Cass isn't even there, is he? And if he doesn't like it, then maybe he ought to pick up the phone. Come on, Jason, let me do it until he comes back. That's not asking too much, is it?"

He really had no choice. "Fine. Done. What else?"

"I won't stay at your family's house."

He almost laughed at that. There was no way he could get

around the estate in the shape he was in. "Agreed. You'll return to your room at the Bickmore. Anything else?"

"You'll take a look at my short film I've finished," she said softly.

"Okay," he says carefully. "I'm not sure I can help you in any way."

"Jason I didn't ask you to buy it, I asked you to look at it. Will you?"

"Yes," he said. "When can you be here?"

"Let me see. I suppose I have to arrange my own plane?" she asked, and laughed.

"It would be a big help."

"We can not afford all this flying. I'll be there tonight."

"Fantastic. Hey..." He was smiling for the first time in days. "Bring that blue dress."

"You are so bad, Jason Blackthorne," she said. "So we're still doing that, huh?"

"Listen, I don't know what we're doing. I just know that I can't wait to touch you and kiss you and boss you around, and in that order. What if...what if we agree to decide what this is later?"

She giggled. "Great idea. So I'll see you tonight?"

"Yes, thank you. And Mallory?"

"Yeah?"

"Did you take the other job?"

Another long pause. "Not yet."

"Great. See you later."

Jason hung up. He felt so much lighter now.

CHAPTER SIXTEEN

MALLORY WAS PACKING A BAG WHEN INEZ WALKED INTO HER room, blinking at the light, having just awakened. She looked at the clothes on Mallory's bed, then at Mallory. "What are you doing?"

"I'm on my way back to Maine."

Inez picked up a pair of heels. "What happened to athleisure wear?"

"I get a better response in heels," Mallory said with a saucy little wink. She did not do saucy little winks as a rule, but she was riding high from Jason's call. He needed her.

Inez looked at her clothes. "What about the director job?"

"Oh. I emailed Kelly and told her I couldn't make a decision right now. She said she understood, but to please call her if I change my mind."

Inez stared at her. "You're really, seriously, giving up the chance at a job you've been trying to get for years?"

Mallory didn't look at Inez. "Now is not a good time, that's all."

She could feel the waves of disapproval coming off Inez. "How long will you be gone?"

"Umm…not sure." Mallory looked up. "But he made me a deal. I get to direct some scenes." She grinned.

Inez's eyes widened with surprise. "You amaze me, Mallory. I never thought you, of all people, would be the type to manipulate that situation." She laughed.

Mallory's stomach sank. "Excuse me?"

"What? Are you going to tell me it's a coincidence that your sex life picked up and now you're suddenly directing?"

"It's not like that," Mallory said defensively. "Cass has disappeared and we have to start production. If we don't, we lose money."

"Sure," Inez said, still grinning.

Her attitude annoyed Mallory. Inez knew her better than anyone and knew that was not how Mallory did things. "You don't have to be so jaded," she said curtly.

"You don't have to be naïve," Inez shot back.

Mallory glared at her roommate as she walked out of her room. "That's not why!" she shouted after her. God, she hoped that was not why.

"I always tell you straight!" Inez shouted back.

Ned was at the King Harbor airport to pick Mallory up. "You're back," he announced.

"I am."

"You going to the estate?" he asked as he tossed her bag into the back.

"To the Bickmore," she said.

Ned's thick brows rose to his hairline. "Fancy," he said. He barreled into town in the white windowless van and up the drive of the Bickmore, coming to such an abrupt halt that Mallory nearly pitched through the windshield.

"Thanks," Mallory said with a bit of a side-eye for his driving. As she climbed out of the van, a bellman hurried out to take her suitcase before she realized what he was doing. She followed him to the counter and dug in her backpack for her wallet. "I believe I should have a reservation—"

"Yes, Ms. Price, we were expecting you."

Well, well, Jason could take care of things like this after all. She was smiling when she opened her wallet. "I've got a card right here."

"That's not necessary, Ms. Price," the man said. "All is arranged. You're on the Blackthorne account." He smiled and handed her the key. "The same room as before. Mr. Blackthorne asked that you go directly to his room when you are settled. He's working there."

"Okay. Thanks." Mallory turned around for her bag, but the bellman had already whisked it away.

Mallory went into her room and looked out the window at the ocean. She could get used to this, traveling by private jet and living in luxury hotels. She smiled to herself. She was a lucky girl right now.

She checked out her appearance, then went down the hall to Jason's room and knocked.

"It's open!" she heard his familiar voice call.

She turned the crystal knob and pushed the door open, peeking around the corner. When she saw Jason, she made a sound of surprise. "Oh my God, Jason!" she exclaimed as she came into the room. He was lying on the bed in sweats and long sleeve tee, and a knit cap on his head.

"Mallory," he said, his voice full of relief.

"Your back! Surely you've been to see someone about it."

"I have." He tried to shift, but it clearly pained him.

"Don't move," she said, coming forward. She grabbed

some pillows and helped him lean up. "What's going on with your back?"

"According to the doctor, it's either a herniated disk or maybe an autoimmune disease."

"No way!"

"I've got some tests scheduled for next week and in the meantime, I've got some muscle relaxers and pain pills." He smiled grimly. "You'll have to drive."

"Poor Jason," she said with true sympathy.

He sighed and laced his fingers with hers. "I'm glad you're here."

Oh, be still her heart. "Me too."

"Come here," he said softly, and pulled her down to kiss her. "I'm *really* glad you're here," he said again, and kissed her cheek, then let her go. "Let's get to work. Do you see my phone anywhere? And can you give me a hand up out of this bed?"

She helped him up, and when he was on his feet, he smiled down at her, pushing hair from her temple. "We need to go to the hospital and see the set-up. We've got the site for two days. We have to start filming tomorrow. The crew is finishing the set-up tonight."

"Okay."

"Are you ready?"

"Never been readier," she said, and smiled when he kissed her forehead.

It was excruciating to watch Jason get in the Range Rover. The pain was etched around his mouth and eyes. Mallory thought he ought not to be driving around, but she could also tell by the furrow between his eyes that now was not the time to bring it up.

At the hospital, the crew was hard at work. It never ceased to amaze Mallory how many people it took to bring a project to the screen. All of this was to film Trent walking out the hospital, his character having received the news that his estranged son's best friend had been killed.

Neil was on set, and greeted Mallory with a smile. "Great to see you," he said, and to Jason, "Where the hell is Cass?"

"I'm not sure," Jason said. "He won't answer his phone."

Neil stared at Jason. "We have our first shoot tomorrow."

"Right. Meet your director," he said, and nodded at Mallory.

"Surprise!" Mallory said sheepishly.

"No way," Neil said.

"It's true," Jason said.

Neil sighed. He nodded and looked at Mallory. "Okay, kid. Let's do this."

Mallory didn't want to turn into a complete nerd in front of everyone, but the next two hours was absolute heaven to her. She and Neil went over the scene, walking the location set, looking at different angles, and determining, together, the camera placement. He actually listened to her. And he showed her different ways to look at the scene.

She and Jason had a quick meal, but Jason was clearly ready to return to his room and take a pain killer. Mallory turned in early, too.

She was on set at five the next morning.

When she talked to her sister later than night, Mallory could not adequately describe how her first day on the job had gone. It was magic, so fantastic, so much of what she had always dreamed, that the usual superlatives seemed ridiculously inept. Mallory had felt alive. She had felt like this day, and the direction she had done with Trent on something as simple as walking out of the hospital, was the thing she was put on this earth to do. At the end of a sixteen-hour day, she had boundless energy. She couldn't wait to get back out there.

Jason actually laughed at her when she joined him in his room for dinner and told him the same. "This is what I am meant to do," she said excitedly. "This is in my blood."

"You are really excited," he said, and shook his head to the wine that had been delivered with dinner.

"I've said "action" before in my short films, but today, it felt…it felt real, Jason. It felt like I am this person. Like I am finally getting somewhere."

"You're good at this," Jason said.

Mallory beamed at him. "Thank you. So are you." It felt like they were a team. Like they'd been producing shows together for years.

"I'm serious. You've got great instincts. Neil thinks so, too. And you're much more pleasant to work with than Cass, so that's a big bonus."

She laughed. "I listen to him. I'm learning a lot from him, honestly. Leaning on him if you want to know the truth."

"That's great. Take advantage of his experience."

Mallory was learning from everyone. She was creating entertainment, and she was in love with life.

And Jason.

Yes, she was falling in love with him. He was part of this —a huge part of this perfect life she was suddenly living. He was warm and creative and he was supportive. That night, they watched episode three of the first season and as Mallory pointed things out, he agreed with her.

He agreed with her and she didn't hate it.

She knew Jason was worried about the production, but she hoped Cass never came back. It was odd—he'd disappeared from the production, but he hadn't actually resigned. And he was still giving interviews about Darien. Mallory couldn't figure out what his end game was.

As for Darien, a woman had recently come forward

claiming Darien had raped her ten years ago, and the media attention had turned to the war of words between her and Darien. Which meant away from *Bad Intentions* and Blackthorne Entertainment. Mallory was aware that Blackthorne Enterprises was still concerned about the situation, but Mallory was too wrapped in her own world to pay much attention to those phone calls.

She didn't mention going back to L.A., and Jason didn't either. After the hospital scenes, they would be filming the warehouse scenes.

After her third day on set, Mallory called Inez to tell her she'd be a few more days.

"You sound giddy," Inez said.

"Inez, I am not kidding when I say this is the best time of my life I've ever had. Ever! It's all coming together. I've got the job, I've got the guy." She had to pause a moment to swallow down the insane fit of giggles building in her. "I feel like I've been on this path for so long, and against all odds, it's happening."

"That's wonderful, Mallory. Really," Inez said, and Mallory could tell she meant it sincerely.

Jason's back improved slightly, and one night, he convinced her to go to the estate and meet his grandmother. "I need to check on her," he said.

Fiona—Nana—invited them in. Her house smelled like fresh baked bread. Her white hair was newly coiffed, and she'd put on button-up jeans and a cable-knit sweater for the evening. Over bowls of homemade clam chowder, Fiona delighted Mallory with a tale about Jason when he was a boy. "It was Phillip's birthday," she said. "We'd all gathered as we did for all the boys' birthdays. We thought Jason was playing baseball. Oh, he loved baseball, did you know that?"

"I didn't," Mallory said, sharing a smile with Jason.

"Well, we waited and waited and he didn't come home. Graham and Claire were so worried. They kept asking the boys, 'are you sure he was at school?' They said they thought he was."

Jason snorted. "I wasn't exactly on anyone's radar."

"Where were you?" Mallory asked.

"Oh, he finally came strolling home. He'd been to the movies."

Jason looked at Mallory. "*Star Wars*."

"Oh," she said. "Which one?"

"Phantom Menace."

"An excellent reason to miss the birthday," she said.

"That's where Jason always was—watching movies. He just buried himself in his room with movies."

Jason's phone pinged. "It was a way to cope, Nana." He glanced at his phone.

"Well, I know that," Nana said. "It was your aunt and uncle who didn't understand it."

Mallory watched curiously as Jason slid the phone back into his pocket.

"I needed the escape after losing Mom and Dad."

"Me too," Mallory said. "I mean, I needed the escape."

"Oh dear, did you lose your parents, too?" Nana asked.

Mallory waved her hand. "No, no—they are very much alive. But they weren't around much and they weren't big on parenting."

"Well that's odd," Nana said.

Mallory couldn't help but laugh. "It was." She glanced at Jason. He gave her a hint of a smile—he understood.

They finished the meal with more family tales, and when they had finished, Mallory carried the bowls to the kitchen. "Nana, we need to get going," Jason said.

"Leave that, Mallory," Nana said. "Gives me something

to do. Now you come back to see me, will you?" she asked, taking Mallory's hands in hers.

"I'd love to," Mallory said.

Jason had to dip in an odd way to kiss his grandmother's cheek—his back wouldn't bend like it should. "I'll see you in a couple of days," he said. He held Mallory's hand to the car.

He drove, claiming his painkillers had kicked in. On the way back to the Bickmore, he put his hand on her knee. "I have an idea what we can do next," he said.

"Is it forbidden?" Mallory asked.

"So forbidden," he agreed, and squeezed her knee.

"I'm in," she said.

"Great. I just have to make a quick phone call first." He removed his hand from her knee.

"More trouble?" she asked.

"I don't know. Uncle Graham has been trying to get hold of me."

When they reached the Bickmore, the valet took the car from Jason. Mallory wrapped her arm around his waist. "I'm not an invalid," he protested.

"You move like one," she said.

They were laughing at his zombie-like walk as they eased in through the front door. Mallory didn't see Cass at first, not until he stood up and blocked their path with his girth.

It was bad enough that seeing the specter of Cass made Mallory's heart sink. But he was not alone.

CHAPTER SEVENTEEN

CASS FROWNED DISAPPROVINGLY AT MALLORY BEFORE turning that disapproving glare to Jason.

"So you came back," Jason said curtly. The lack of professionalism galled him, and by the look of things, Cass was up to no good. "Who's your friend?"

"Who, him?" Cass looked at the young man. "This is Davis Markham. He is an investigative reporter."

Jason had never wanted to kill a man with his bare hands, but he did in that moment. He might have done it, too, if he could have moved without being driven to his knees in pain. He looked at Mallory—her expression of sick astonishment mirrored what he felt. He knew, instinctively, that Graham's calls had something to do with this, and he needed to handle it. "Why don't you go ahead and I'll join you in a moment," he said softly.

Mallory blinked. "Maybe I should—"

"Please."

"Yes, be a good little girl and run on, Mallory," Cass drawled.

She snapped her gaze to him. "You know what, Cass?"

"No, what?" he sneered.

She looked like she was going to launch herself at him. Jason reached for her hand, but she took one look at Mr. Davis Markham, and abruptly pivoted about, striding away.

Cass chuckled. "Shall we sit?" he asked pleasantly, and pointed to a settee.

There was no way Jason could sit on that settee. "Over here," he said, and hobbled to a tall table with barstools he could slide onto.

"What's wrong with you?" Cass asked. "Why are you walking like that?"

"Never mind," Jason muttered.

Cass arranged himself on a stool. The young man stood. "Davis and I have been talking about Darien's problem," Cass said, as if they were catching up on old friends.

Jason said nothing.

"You remember Candice Herrera, do you not?"

Candice Herrera was an actress who had read for the part of the ex-wife. She didn't get the part. As Jason recalled, she interpreted the role as if the character was a mob boss, not a woman scorned. "What about her?"

"She had accused Darien of molesting her," Cass said easily, without any sort of emotion that Jason could detect.

This was news to Jason. He was uncomfortably aware of the reporter watching him. His phone began to ping again. He didn't have to look to know it was Uncle Graham.

"Not sure where you're going with this, Cass."

"Candice is filing a lawsuit."

Jason clenched his jaw in a supreme effort to remain silent.

"Here is the interesting part," he said, almost gleefully. "She says you knew of it, and you hired Darien anyway. She was forced to decline the role. She lost work because you were coddling a sex offender."

This was staggeringly unbelievable. What was Cass doing? Was his ego so fucking fragile that he would go to such lengths? Did he want out of a contract so bad as this? If he did, why didn't he just say so?

"What do you say to that charge, Mr. Blackthorne?" the reporter asked him.

"That there is absolutely no truth to it. Now, if you will excuse me, I have a call to take."

He got up and walked away as best he could, his back screaming at him with every step. Davis Markham shouted, "Did you know Darien Simmons was a sexual predator, Mr. Blackthorne?"

"Oh, and by the way, Jason," Cass called out. "I quit. I won't be associated with a film company that hires sex offenders."

Jason could not believe that douche. He should have terminated their agreement the moment he wouldn't take Jason's calls, but he hadn't, because in the back of his head he feared another potential lawsuit and the stain on the Black-thorne name.

His phone began to ping again. He dug it out of his pocket as he managed his way up the stairs, sweat pouring down his back. It was over. He punched the button on the phone. "Hi, Uncle Graham. I know why you're calling. I was just waylaid at the Bickmore."

"Good God," Uncle Graham said. "That's why I was trying to get hold of you. To warn you. Jason, this has gotten out of control—"

"Look, I know," Jason said. "But please don't do anything, Uncle Graham. If you pull funding it looks like it's true, and you have to believe me, I didn't know anything about Darien Simmons."

"I believe you, Jason, that is not the point. The point is we are facing a rash of lawsuits."

"I have insurance," Jason said quickly. Not enough, he figured, but still. "I can fix this. It's already turning into a he-said she-said, and Cass…well, I don't know what his problem is, but he's trying to destroy me."

"What? Why?"

"Because he wants a better deal with Sony Pictures. If he can get out of his obligation to me, he can pursue it. But he can't walk away without cause without losing money. And honestly? I think also because I brought a young woman on who is better at the job than he is and he doesn't like it."

Uncle Graham didn't speak, so Jason jumped into the silence. "Look, Cass is gone. I'll get a new director in, right away, just like I did the actor. Someone with some heft, right? We've already started filming. If you pull out now, I won't have enough to cover the last few episodes. I need you to believe in me, Uncle Graham. For once in my life, I need you to believe in me."

Uncle Graham made a sound of surprised. "Jason…I have *always* believed in you. *Always.* You are so talented and so creative. This is not a reflection on you. I'm proud of what you've done. My brother would be bursting with pride if he could see you now. This is just business."

Jason stopped at the top of the stairs. "It's not just business to me, Uncle Graham. It's my life."

Uncle Graham was silent for what seemed an eternity. Jason said nothing. He'd said all there was to say.

"All right," Uncle Graham said. "Just…just get this taken care of."

Jason closed his eyes and sent up a silent prayer of

thanks. "Thanks, Uncle Graham. I won't let you down, I promise."

He clicked off the call. He looked back—Cass and the reporter had left. He turned around and made his way to Mallory's door.

She answered after one knock. Her eyes were wide, her face ashen. "What happened?"

"Can I come in?" Jason asked, and hobbled into her room, easing himself down on her bed and onto his back. He filled her in on what had transpired downstairs. Her face turned whiter as he talked. When he'd finished telling her most of it, she sank onto the bed beside him.

"Is he…is he coming back to work?"

Jason snorted. "No. He quit."

"Oh." She looked up. "*Oh.*" A sheepish smile flickered across her face. "I can't say I'm sorry, Jason. He didn't want this gig. I don't know why he didn't quit before."

"Money," Jason said. His back was killing him. Was it possible it was stress related? He'd been feeling better today, until Cass showed up. "I talked to my uncle. He's not pulling funding yet."

"That's good."

He began to clench and unclench his fist against the pain in his back. "I need you to get some directors in for me to interview," he said. His mind was racing ahead, searching for ideas to put a finger in the crack of this dam. "At least three, but they need to be directors who have some notable experience behind them. I need someone who is respected in the industry, who Emmy voters won't write off as being too…" He tried to think of the word and happened to look up and see Mallory's face.

She looked like she'd been hit by a truck. Her expression was crumpled, her eyes bewildered, and Jesus, he could be an idiot at times. He struggled to sit up. "Mallory, listen—"

She was already off the bed. "Why not me?" she demanded of him. "I'm not going to pretend to be okay with this, Jason. I have to know—why not me?"

"You're too green," he said honestly. "I need someone with clout."

"Why? Everyone on set has clout. You've got the best in the business, and you can't let someone new in?"

He could feel her distress. She wished she could feel his. There was so much riding on this series. He couldn't hand this to her because he loved her.

The thought caught him off guard. He did love her. But he had worked hard to get here, to this point of his career. "Not this time," he said softly.

Mallory's gaze dropped to the floor. She was taking in deep gulps of air to calm herself.

"Will you hear me out?" he begged her.

"No. I don't need to."

"This isn't just about you, Mallory. You cannot understand the pressure I'm under. How much I have riding on this. My investors are my *family*, and they are threatening to pull out if I can't produce a quality project. I have worked just as hard as you to get where I am, and I can't afford to lose the confidence of the studio by installing someone brand-new into the director's chair. You have to be reasonable about this."

"You don't think I can make quality," she said quietly.

"Of course I do," he said gruffly. "It's not that. It's a matter of moving quickly with the best people—"

"You don't think I'm the best people," she said.

"I think you are the best people, Mallory. But I don't know if you are the best director. You've done a couple of short films and directed three exterior scenes at a hospital. That's not a lot to go on. Please try and understand."

She looked up and pinned him with a look. "Actually, I think I understand really well." Her eyes were shining with tears. "I think I've always understood, but I was so stupid that I...I..." She dropped her head again.

"You what?"

"Fell in love with you." Her shoulders slumped. "I am such an idiot."

"No. No you're not. Jesus Christ woman, can't you see that I love you, too?" he asked, struggling to his feet. "I can't do anything without you."

"Right. You need someone to find your phone and help you out of bed when you throw your back out, and oh, fly to Maine at the drop of a hat and do what Cass was supposed to do for a fraction of the cost, and what else, Jason? What else can you not do without me?"

Her words were daggers. He felt slightly nauseous with the hint of truth in it, but it was more than that. He loved her. They were cut from the same cloth. "That's not fair."

Mallory shrugged. She walked to the door and opened it. "I think you should go to your room."

"Mallory, let's talk about this."

She wouldn't look at him. "Please," she said.

Jason walked to the door. He paused there and looked down at her. She was clearly fighting to maintain her composure. But when she lifted her head, she looked him square in the eye and said, "Consider this my two week notice."

Jason was gutted. It was the death knell to him, to his show, to his life. "Don't do this."

"I'm doing what I should have done a long time ago. I am never going to be anything but coffee girl if I don't stand up for myself and take the opportunities where I can get them.

I'll finish the hospital scenes tomorrow and get you some directors, but then I'm leaving, Jason." She pulled the door open wider.

Everything was falling down around his head and screaming into the pain in his back. Jason could not remember feeling so incredibly frustrated as he did now, and did something he'd never done in his life—he took a swing at the wall. It served nothing other than to make the pain in his back almost send him to his knees. He gasped, put his hand on the doorjamb to keep from sliding to the floor.

Mallory didn't ask him if he was all right. She said, "You ought to be more careful," and folded her arms over her middle.

Through gritted teeth, Jason said, "I can't fight you right now, Mallory. As much as I want to duke this out with you, I can't. But we're not done." He hobbled out. The sound of her door closing behind him reverberated through his entire body.

CHAPTER EIGHTEEN

MALLORY EMAILED KELLY AT MORNING MOONLIGHT FILMS from the last private plane trip she would ever take. She couldn't believe how many she'd taken—she was singlehandedly destroying the environment.

She received an almost-instant email response: *FANTASTIC. Please come in Monday to discuss.*

When Mallory dragged her bag in through the door of her apartment, Inez was lounging on the couch, in the middle of a *Real Housewives of New York* marathon. She sat up, surprised to see Mallory. "I thought you were going to be gone a few more days. What's up? Wait, I know—you came to get evening wear." She laughed.

Mallory dropped her backpack and covered her face with her hands.

"Hey!" Inez leaped from the couch, put her arms around Mallory and dragged her to the couch to sit. "What's the matter? What happened? Wait. Let me get a couple of beers."

Mallory hardly drank her beer at all while Inez drank two, listening with rapt attention to everything that had happened in Maine, up until the moment she'd stepped foot on the private plane. "You were right, Inez. You were so right. *Again.*"

"Oh Mallory. You didn't do his laundry did you?" she asked.

"Sort of."

Inez nodded thoughtfully.

"You hate him right?" Mallory asked weakly.

"With the strength of a thousand burning suns," she said adamantly. "But…" She winced a little.

"But? But what?"

"But don't hate me…but he kind of has a point, doesn't he?" she asked.

Mallory stared at her best friend.

"Hear me out," Inez said.

"I don't want to hear you out," Mallory said.

"You've never done anything like that," Inez said. "And, you know, a few scenes is great, and you can put it on your resume. But the story arc is over thirteen chapters and who knows how many scenes, and all that goes into it. That's a *lot* Mallory."

"I just said I don't want to hear you out," she said peevishly.

"And Jason might think you're the greatest thing since Scorsese, but he's right about this. He's got to have someone with experience who can film this in an emergency and make it look great."

Mallory sank lower onto the couch. She knew what Inez was saying was right. The thought had certainly crossed her mind several times. But she was still hurt. "Why is everyone against me?"

"No one is against you. Look, it's all paying off. You have directed a few scenes, which, you know, was your goal. You have an interview on Monday. It's all going to work out.

Trust me. I always tell you straight."

But it wasn't all going to work out. She didn't disagree with Inez, really. But there was one thing Inez was leaving out—Mallory was in love with Jason. But she had to leave.

The new director with "heft," Jeff Craig, wanted to throw out all the production design and start over. He had a completely different idea of how the second season ought to look. Neil, the director of photography, and Maleeka, the production designer, and Jason met in L.A. to go over the new plan. Jason managed to slip into a neurosurgeon he knew and get a steroid shot in his back. He felt 1000 percent better. But the doctor warned he'd have to have surgery at some point.

He'd get right on that—just as soon as the second season was in the can and the Emmy nominations were announced.

His head was much clearer about things, and although Jeff's ideas constituted a production delay, Jason and Neil and Maleeka were in agreement—it was the way to go. Jason didn't know what he did with the meticulous notes he made, but he could remember most of it. Jeff didn't have a signed contract yet, but wanted to hit the ground running. "Just let my agent know the terms," Jeff said.

There was one term Jason wasn't sure about. He needed to talk to someone who wasn't involved with Blackthorne Entertainment. He picked up the phone and called his cousin Ross. He was not quite a year older than Ross, and they'd been buddies growing up.

"Hey," Ross said when he answered the phone. "Long time, bro. What's up?"

"How are you, Ross?" Jason asked. Ross was a race-car driver, and recently, he'd been involved in an awful crash.

The miraculous thing was, he'd walked away without a scratch. Ross had always seemed fearless to Jason, a true risk-taker. Jason needed to be fearless right now, so Ross seemed the perfect person to talk to.

"I'm good," Ross said. "Dad's been on my case, but what else is new." He chuckled.

"Have you heard from your mom?"

"Not really. I texted her, and she sent one back that said not to worry about her. That's it." They chatted about the family, and the rift between Uncle Graham and Aunt Claire. Ross had heard of the scandal with Jason's show from Brock, so Jason filled in the blanks for him, updating him on his new hire.

"Sounds like you've got it under control," Ross said. "So what's this call about?"

Jason fidgeted with a pen on his desk. "I may be about to blow it up all over again," he said, and told Ross what he was thinking of doing.

When he'd finished laying it out, Ross just laughed. "Dude, you don't need advice. You need a pep talk. Go get the girl, man!"

"She might be done with me," Jason said morosely.

"If she is, well, at least you know you went down with a fight. Is there really any alternative? You sound like you're in love with her."

Ross could always read Jason pretty well.

Mallory's two weeks was not up yet, but since Jason had come back to L.A., she'd been pretty scarce around the office. He had to dig into the office files to find her address. On his way to her house, he called Jeff Craig. This was the first part that could blow up in his face, and at first, Jason thought it had. Jeff was not happy with what he had to say, and argued with Jason. But after fifteen minutes of Jason patiently explaining himself, Jeff finally hemmed and hawed his way into a tentative agreement. But with conditions.

Next up was Mallory. She would have conditions, too. If she would even listen to him.

He had pulled onto her street when he got a call from Uncle Graham. Jason braced himself, ready to defend his latest decisions. The cost overruns were beginning to mount.

"Good morning, Jason," Uncle Graham said pleasantly. "How's the weather in sunny California?"

"Sunny," Jason said. "How is it up your way?"

"Good sailing weather. Have you seen the most recent entertainment news?"

Jason braced himself. "No, I've been on the phone. What now?"

"Well," Uncle Graham said with a giddiness that startled Jason, "a video has surfaced of one Miss Candice Herrera and Mr. Cass Farenthold having a little conspiracy meeting at a Starbuck's in New York."

"What?"

"A customer sitting next to them recognized them both and videoed their conversation. They planned the whole thing to get him out of his contract without penalty, and get her a little money. He wanted to make it look like he had to leave because of your poor judgment in hiring."

Jason was stunned. Nothing should surprise him anymore, and yet, everything did.

"The good news is, I've instructed our attorney to speak with your attorney, Jason. You've got a very good defamation lawsuit you can file. Just wait until you see the video."

"I don't even know what to say."

"Say you'll get this production rolling and reduce the overruns," Uncle Graham said jovially.

"I will, Uncle Graham," Jason assured him as he pulled

up outside an apartment building in Studio City. "There is just one last thing I have to do to get it all nailed down."

They said their goodbyes, and Jason sat a moment in his car, going over what he would say. For the thousandth time in his life, he wished he could organize his thoughts a little better. He wasn't quite sure where to start with Mallory. He needed Mallory to organize his speech to Mallory.

He found the apartment and knocked on the door. A very pretty woman with long black hair opened the door. She also had lovely expressive brown eyes, because they were radiating surprise and disgust at him. "Umm...I'm Jason—"

"I know who you are." She glanced over her shoulder. "Mallory is busy right now."

"No, she's not," Jason said calmly. "I don't know what she's told you, but I've come here to make it right."

"Really?" She folded her arms. "Because—"

"Inez?"

Mallory appeared in the hallway behind the woman whose name, apparently, was Inez. "What are you doing? *Jason?*"

"He's going to give you some song and dance, Mallory," Inez said.

Mallory was staring at Jason. She looked confused. She looked beautiful. She looked like she'd missed him as much as he'd missed her, but that might have been a whole lot of wishful thinking on his part. She stepped up, nudging her friend out of the way. "Don't you have to get to set?" she asked as she studied Jason.

"Not for an hour."

Mallory turned her gaze away from Jason and stared at her friend.

"Fine," Inez said. She disappeared into the apartment, and Jason could hear things banging around.

"How are you?" he asked.

"Okay," she said, a little uncertainly. "You?"

"Good."

"Your back?"

"I got a steroid shot."

Inez reappeared with a bag slung over her shoulder. She glared at Jason as she went out. "Don't let him sweet talk you," she said darkly to Mallory.

"I won't," Mallory said, her gaze on Jason. "Come in." She turned and walked down the hall.

Jason followed her into a living area painted powder blue. He could see a community pool sparkling through the sliding glass doors. The room was neatly kept, of course. There were some books stacked on a coffee table. Very colorfully embroidered pillows on the couch.

Mallory did not sit. Neither did Jason. "Sooo," she said.

"I hired a new director. Jeff Craig."

She frowned. She released the breath she was apparently holding. "He's the best."

"Yeah," Jason said, nodding. "He wants a complete production redesign, though."

"I don't blame him."

"We're officially behind schedule now."

She frowned. "Let me guess. You need me to rework on the schedules before I go."

"I need you, Mallory," he said, his words heartfelt. "But not for that. I didn't come here for that, obviously."

"Then why did you come?"

"To talk. To explain."

"You don't need to explain," she said, and looked to the window and the pool beyond.

"I do. I couldn't offer you the position of director. I stand by that decision. You need more experience before you can tackle a project like this."

"I know," she said softly.

"But I can't ignore your goals, either. When you love someone, you can't ignore that."

Her gaze snapped back to him. "What?"

"I told Jeff that as a condition of contract, he must agree to hire you as an assistant director."

"*What?*" She looked incredulous.

"Jeff didn't want to. He said he had plenty of assistants. But I told him that was the deal, that it was incumbent on us to develop female directors where we could. But that I couldn't hire you."

"You can't?" her voice sounded weaker.

"According to my assistant, that would be fraternization. I can't love you and be your boss at the same time, Mallory."

She was staring at him in utter disbelief.

"I know you've probably told the corporate film people you'll go to work there, but that's not what you want, is it? You want a shot at directing dramas. I know you do because I watched your contest entries and you're *good*, Mallory, you are so good. But there are rough edges. With some training, some study under a guy like Jeff, you can become a really fantastic director. I said as much to Jeff. So will Neil—he thinks you're talented, too."

"What…what did Jeff say?" she asked tentatively.

"He said he'd like to meet you. And he had a couple of conditions. He can use you in the way he sees fit, for one. And if it's not working out, he can let you go. That's only fair."

Mallory's mouth gaped with surprise.

Jason moved forward. He reached for her hand. "I know I disappointed you. I know I let you down. It wasn't the right fit, and if I'd done it, I would have been giving you an opportunity you hadn't earned only because I love you."

"You really love me?"

He wished he could adequately express how much he did love her. He'd thought about it a lot the last few days. "I love you, Mallory. I think I have since the first day you organized my inbox and then told me that you would not tolerate the break room in its present condition, and by the way, there was great new software for creating call sheets."

She smiled. Her eyes began to glisten. "I can't believe this is happening."

"I love you, and I just hope you can learn to love me."

"Jason I—"

"You don't have to say anything. I just needed to get that off my chest."

"But I love you, too, Jason. I have loved you since I first saw you and you asked me that ridiculous question about how to use the Find my Phone feature. I loved you when you were unreasonable and impossible, and there was never a day, not one, that I didn't want to strangle you and then rip your clothes off."

"Oh. Wow. That's love I guess," he said uncertainly.

"It is. It is deep love, Jason Blackthorne. And you were right. I didn't want to hear it, and it hurt my feelings, but you were right. I'm not ready to direct a series. I know that. But I also knew I had to quit. If I didn't, I'd be organizing your inbox for the rest of my life."

He pulled her closer, put his arm around her waist and drew her into his body. "I don't care about my inbox. I only care that you are with me. I do need you, Mallory. But I need you for me. Not the job."

She smiled up at him, lifted up on her toes and kissed him. "This is a freaking fairy tale. I used to read about them

at the library, and now here I am, right in the middle of one."
She grinned and kissed him again.

"You know what happens at the end of a fairy tale, right?"
Jason asked, and nuzzled her neck, so happy to have her back
in his arms.

"A happy ever after?" she asked, and nibbled his ear.

"Before that."

"Crazy, wild, sex?" She bit his ear.

"I thought you'd never ask."

Mallory laughed. She grabbed his hand and tugged him to
her bedroom and their happily ever after.

THE END

ABOUT THE AUTHOR

Julia London is the *New York Times,* *USA Today,* and *Publisher's Weekly* best-selling author of more than forty romantic fiction novels. She is the author of the critically acclaimed *Highland Grooms* historical series, including *The Devil in Tartan, Tempting the Laird* and *Seduced by a Scot.* She is also the author of several contemporary romances, including *Suddenly in Love, Suddenly Dating, Suddenly Engaged* and *Suddenly Single,* as well as the upcoming *The Charmer in Chaps* and *The Devil in the Saddle,* the first two books in the *Princes of Texas* series.

Julia is the recipient of the RT Bookclub Award for Best Historical Romance and a six-time finalist for the prestigious RITA award for excellence in romantic fiction.

She lives in Austin, Texas.

 facebook.com/JuliaLondonAuth

 twitter.com/juliaflondon

instagram.com/julia_f_london

Made in the USA
Columbia, SC
26 September 2019